The Alchemy

You can't change the e...
can you?

When Charlotte and I...
they are horrified at the ...
lured to his death, and o... ...g they—
the readers—can do.

But the alchemy set changes all that. When Charlotte
and David realize it can work magic, they decide to
conjure up the world of the book and go in to warn the
prince. But it's not as easy as all that. And when they get
into the world of the book, they find things are different.
Whom can they trust? Who is real? And will they reach
the prince in time?

WEEM WHITAKER spent his childhood in rural North
Yorkshire before going to Cambridge to read Classics.
After doing research in ancient philosophy, he moved
back to the hamlet where he grew up, and now lives
there with his wife. He enjoys walking in the local
countryside, which provides part of the inspiration for
his writing. *The Alchemy Set* is his first novel.

The Alchemy Set

The Alchemy Set

Weem Whitaker

Oxford University Press

Oxford New York Toronto

Oxford University Press, Great Clarendon Street, Oxford OX2 6DP

Oxford New York
Athens Auckland Bangkok Bogota Buenos Aires
Calcutta Cape Town Chennai Dar es Salaam
Delhi Florence Hong Kong Istanbul Karachi
Kuala Lumpur Madrid Melbourne
Mexico City Mumbai Nairobi Paris Sao Paulo
Singapore Taipei Tokyo Toronto Warsaw

and associated companies in
Berlin Ibadan

Oxford is a trade mark of Oxford University Press

Copyright © Weem Whitaker 1998
First published 1998

A CIP catalogue record for this book is available
from the British Library

Cover illustration by Neil Reed

ISBN 0 19 271767 7

Printed and bound in Great Britain by
Biddles Ltd, Guildford and King's Lynn

For Katie

Contents

CHAPTER I

A Drowning

' "Come!" called the Sprite, and she slipped back over the surface of the water, smiling and beckoning. Her voice drew Prince Roland on. He glanced down at the mossy rock on which he stood, which sloped steeply down into the darkness of the Tarn. Still the Sprite hung back, teasing and calling to him to follow. He took another step forward, and just as the pale, watery face glided almost up to his own, his foot began to slip. He was sliding now, down, down into the Tarn, while the face melted away with a bubble of laughter. A fountain was playing where the Sprite had been; it swept around him in a torrent, and cold, strong arms carried him down below the water. That was the end of his hopes, and the end of his quest. Down and down he sank, and the Thing that lived below ate the flesh off his bones." '

David finished reading. They were in Charlotte's room, which looked out over the road. For a while they sat in silence, with only the sound of traffic going by outside. Then Charlotte said, 'That's awful.'

'Grim,' agreed David.

'Is that really the end of the book?'

'There's nothing more but a few blank pages.'

'But why drowning? It's just so . . . ugly. And he trusted her: he trusted her and then she drowned him!'

'I know.'

'Well, *I* wouldn't have been taken in,' Charlotte declared.

'You would, though,' said David, 'if you were all alone in those woods, and had to save your princess, stolen away under the water by the Thing. The Sprite looked like a friend.'

'But he must have known she was tricking him. He must have done!'

'I don't think it's so easy knowing when people are tricking you.'

Charlotte heaved a deep sigh and looked down at her lap. David let the book drop by his side on the rug. They both sat in silence, pondering gloomily.

Just then their mother poked her head around the door.

'Finished reading? How did it come out?'

The children looked up at her bleakly. 'He got killed,' said David.

Mum looked surprised. 'Oh. That's a pity.'

'But, Mum, he was drowned!' Charlotte wailed. 'By someone he trusted! The Sprite promised she'd help him, and then she killed him!'

'It's only a story, Charlotte. It isn't real.'

'How do you know?' retorted Charlotte.

'Well . . . I just do. Stories are only made up. No one's been drowned really.'

'But he *has* been drowned. He has!' Charlotte insisted.

Mum squatted down beside them on the floor. 'Look, here's what you do. Why don't the two of you make up an ending of your own? Make it come out some other way—the way you think it ought to. How about that?' She was smiling at them, but Charlotte had her eyes on the rug, and David was frowning in thought.

'But that's how it's written,' he objected. 'You can't just change it like that.'

Mum drew in a deep breath. 'Well, people do get drowned sometimes, David. Things don't always work out just the way you'd like them to. You wait till you get out into the real world: then you'll know what I mean.' She smiled again, and stood up. 'Now then, why don't you do something else, to take your minds off it? What about your homework?'

'We've done it,' said David.

'Then you could go outdoors. It's a nice Saturday.'

David looked at his sister, who was still staring at the rug. 'What about it?'

'S'pose we could,' Charlotte mumbled.

'We could always have a look round the junk shop,' David went on, brightening slightly, 'couldn't we, Mum?'

Mum pursed her lips. 'I was thinking of somewhere *nice*, like the park.'

'We'll have to cross the park anyway to get to the junk shop,' David pointed out innocently.

Mum flapped her arms by her side. 'All right. Just wash your hands when you get back, that's all. And take care crossing the road.'

'Come on then, Charlotte,' said David. They got to their feet, and David gathered his pocket money together just in case of any specially interesting junk. Then they set off. It was May, and warm. In the park, there were lots of people out lying on the grass or playing games, but David and Charlotte plodded along in silence.

'Fancy thinking you could change the way the book came out just by pretending,' Charlotte said after a while. 'Mum ought to know better than that.'

'Grown-ups never understand about real and pretend,' said David.

Soon they reached the other side of the park, passed

the row of bollards, and carried on up the street the junk shop was on. In front of the grubby shop-front they paused.

'Well?' said David. 'Shall we?'

'We might as well, as long as we're here,' said Charlotte.

They stepped inside. Normally they could spend hours in the junk shop, browsing among bins and racks overflowing with odds and ends of every sort. There were old coins and chipped cups, door-knockers and pot-stands, buttons and bedknobs. No end of fun could be had thinking up uses for some of the stranger items, trying to guess what they had been for and who had owned them.

''Morning, kids,' said the junkman from behind his counter. The children said hello, and threaded their way down one of the aisles between overhanging towers of junk. Charlotte stopped at a box of oddments whose common theme seemed to be plumbing. She picked up one of the taps and turned the knob at the top, which had an enamel plaque in the middle saying 'Cold'. But the tap made her think of water, and water made her think of drowning. She put it down with a shudder.

Meanwhile David had toured the shop from one end to the other, but nothing held his interest. All the junk looked alike today, and none of it had any story to tell. He came back to his sister's side and heaved a deep sigh.

Charlotte turned to the junkman. 'Haven't you anything new in? Something interesting?'

'I don't know what's wrong with you kids today,' said the junkman. 'Normally you'd've been nattering away by now, arguing about whose bathtub that tap was off. Well, I've got some jigsaw puzzles in, if that's any use. Do you 'em for fifty pence.'

4

'Are there any pieces missing?' asked David, without much enthusiasm.

'' Course there's pieces missing. Wouldn't be junk else, would they? And there's a chemistry set, too.'

'Oh?'

'Under those bits of cloth. Just drop 'em. There.'

Between them, the children pulled out a largish wooden box, very much stained and scratched and battered. It had a torn paper label stuck on its lid with faded curly writing on.

' "Chemy set",' David read off the label. The top of the box slid off, and inside they found an array of dusty glass bottles. Each one was bedded in straw in a separate compartment, and labelled in tiny, curling letters. Next to the bottles there was a ragged, tattered book. Its cover was missing, and it was filled with yet more spidery writing.

'It looks awfully old,' said Charlotte.

'We could buy it and make something smelly,' said David, his interest in life reawakening somewhat. 'Do you think it'll do explosions?'

'Shouldn't think it'll do anything whatever,' said the junkman. 'The chemicals will have gone off long ago. But I'll sell you it for a quid.'

They looked down at the set again. It was certainly something out of the ordinary, and nothing like the chemistry sets they had seen in shops, with neat test tubes nestling in polystyrene. Their eyes met.

'Go shares on it, then?' said David, and Charlotte nodded. He handed the coin to the junkman, and took the set under his arm.

'Good luck,' the junkman chuckled as they picked their way towards the door. 'If I hear any bangs, I'll know it's you.'

When they were halfway home, Charlotte said, 'It won't do anything though, will it?'

'You can't tell,' David argued. 'We might as well try: it's better than moping.'

They were silent for the rest of the way home. Upstairs, they paused on the landing.

'Whose room?' said David.

'Yours, if explosions are on offer.'

David led the way, put the box on the floor, and sat down beside it. Charlotte heaved a deep sigh, and watched while David slid off the lid and began unpacking the bottles from their straw. Then she picked up the lid and peered at the faded writing on the label.

'Don't you think it's odd how the label says "chemy set" and not "chemistry set"?' she mused.

'I think it's an odd thing all round,' replied her brother. 'Just look at these bottles!' He held one up and dusted it off. The glass was bubbled and swirled, and inside there was an amber liquid with gold flakes floating in it. ' "Orpiment",' he read from the label on the side. 'What does that mean?'

'What do *any* of them mean?' wondered Charlotte. She was leaning forward in interest now, and had set up a row of the odd-looking bottles on the rug. Some held powders, dusty yellow or metallic blue, while in others strange shapes swam endlessly in and out of sight through a murky liquid. Their names made unusual reading. There was Atrament and Alkahest, Powder of the Cave, Brimstone and Quicksilver, Green Lion and Shape-Changer. Also there was an egg, carefully wrapped in paper and much too big to be a hen's, with the words *Noli me frangere* written on it in trailing red letters. The children looked at each other. There was

6

nothing left in the box now but the book of instructions, which David now reached out.

'What *have* we got?' Charlotte demanded, while David shook his head, and began puzzling over the twisting script in front of him. The letters looked as if they ought to be familiar, but they always darted off into some strange curlicue or arabesque just as David thought he was on the point of reading them.

'What's the matter?' said Charlotte, as David frowned over the writing.

'I can't make anything of it. It's like Chinese.'

Charlotte crawled round to his side and gazed at the writing. At first the words sprawled meaninglessly over the page. Then all of a sudden they jumped into sensible shapes, and she could read the first line.

' "Ye that will have mastery of this most secret art . . ." ' she began, and David looked at her in surprise. When he glanced back at the book, he too saw the tangled script uncurl, and found himself saying, ' ". . . ye stand at the portal of a maze of perplexity . . ." '

' " . . . wherein lies hid," ' Charlotte finished, ' "the key to the most wondrous art of Alchemy." '

They stared at each other.

'It's an alchemy set!' David burst out. 'That's what it is!'

'What, like potions, and magic, and turning lead into gold?'

'That's right. Look, part of the label must have torn off. It's not a chemy set at all.'

Charlotte was squinting at the writing in the book again. 'What do you think it means, "a maze of perplexity"?'

'I think it means it's going to be horribly difficult and confusing,' said David. He took hold of the book and began to leaf through it.

7

'But none of these chemicals are anything like what we've learnt at school,' said Charlotte, peering at the bottle marked 'Shape-Changer'. Far within its churning depths misty shapes were constantly forming and reforming. 'You don't think it'll do anything, do you?'

'Who knows?' David was now buried in the book of instructions, picking his way slowly through the strange, snakelike lettering. The words writhed into comprehensible outlines just long enough for him to read them, and then lapsed back again into a curly tangle of gibberish.

'Lead into gold . . . there it is! And here's something else: how to turn fantasy into fact.'

'What did you say?' asked Charlotte, looking up from her attempts to see inside the bottle.

'Fantasy into fact,' repeated David. 'Making stories come true.'

'How do you mean, "making them come true"?' demanded Charlotte slowly.

David was frowning over the book. 'Making it the same as real life. Making it so it isn't "just a story", like Mum said.'

Their eyes met, and both seemed to see the face of the prince sinking swiftly down in the grip of the spirit of the waters. Charlotte shivered. 'No thanks. It's bad enough to read about it.'

David said nothing, and peered once more at the book. 'But if it's real,' he began slowly, 'you can go there.'

Charlotte stared at him. 'Well?'

'And if you can go somewhere, you can do things there. Don't you see?'

'You mean *change* things,' said Charlotte, her heart beating fast, 'make them come out different?'

Her brother nodded.

8

'But you couldn't,' Charlotte frowned. 'Books are fixed. They're written some way, and then that's that. They aren't like living in real life.'

'They might be, though, if you made them come true. Maybe it wouldn't mean just living in a groove, the way it was written. And maybe people in books do change things. Who knows?'

'But it won't work, anyway, will it, David?'

David was back buried in the book, reading intently. 'No,' he murmured. 'No, it can't do.' There was a pause.

'How's it *supposed* to work, just supposing it did?' Charlotte asked after a moment.

David scanned back over the page. 'It talks about planting the tree of Mercury . . . it's hard to understand. Listen to this: "Will ye have fact out of fantasy, and tread the land of fable as ye do your own? Then let your work be the taming of Mercury, a spirit wild and wanton, that flits through dreams and tales, and gives them life. This spirit must ye clothe in garments of flesh, and chain to the bonds of earth; for only thus shall ye have your desire."'

David looked up.

'So stories have got a kind of spirit to them, that makes them alive,' puzzled Charlotte. 'And the spirit's called Mercury?'

'I think so . . . ' agreed David slowly. 'But it isn't solid. It's something like a ghost without a body.'

'And you have to give it body,' added Charlotte excitedly. ' "Clothe it in garments of flesh." '

'That's right. Look, it goes on. You plant the tree of Mercury—that means mixing your potion so it's ready to have the book added. You put the book in, and then you add earth and stones, things you can touch and feel.

9

That's the body. And if the fire's just right, and you've mixed them just right, they come together, spirit and body, and your story becomes real.'

David looked up from the book to meet his sister's eyes.

'So you put the book in the potion?' asked Charlotte. 'That's how you make it real?'

David nodded.

'Well, then tear out the last chapter. That way it all comes true but the ending. The Prince goes to the Tarn, he's looking for the Princess, and before the Sprites get hold of him, we turn up and warn him. David! We'll do it!'

'Yes, but hang on a minute, Charlotte. It won't actually work. It must be just a novelty set or something: alchemy isn't real.'

'How do you know?' she retorted.

'Well, for a start, Mercury's not a spirit. It's an element: a metal.'

'That's only what they told us at school. Teachers don't know everything.'

'Besides, the junkman said the chemicals will have gone off.'

'But he doesn't really know. Look at these bottles: some of them look as if they're alive, never mind having gone off.'

She held up the bottle marked 'Shape-Changer', and David gazed into its swirling, blue-green depths. Soon he was lost in its shifting shadows and light, trying in vain to make out the ever-changing shapes.

'See?' said Charlotte. 'At least let's give it a try. Think of the Prince: we could save him!'

'But . . . ' David wrenched his eyes away from the bottle. 'Even so, what if it's dangerous?'

'Why should it be? And what if it is? Prince Roland's *really* in danger. And no one there can do anything about it, because they don't know what's going to happen. They haven't read the book. And no one here but us has got an alchemy set. We've *got* to, David!'

David was thinking hard. 'Mum and Dad'll go spare,' he said at last.

'Oh, we won't be gone long! We'll leave them a note explaining things. Anyhow, we're only doing just what Mum told us to.'

'We're what?'

'She said we should change the ending, and that's what we're doing.'

'Hmm.'

'Oh, come on, David! They'll understand. They've got to.'

'I've an idea they won't, though, even so. Not if we were gone for very long.' David still sat and frowned, while Charlotte was hopping with impatience. Then he looked up with a grin. 'But if we *do* get into the book, we won't be gone for any time at all. Things that happen in books don't take up real time. You know how even if it says "A year passed", it only takes a moment to read?'

'That's right. Of *course* that's right. Oh, David, we'll be back as soon as we've gone, and no one will even know. Oh, come on! We've got to!'

'*If* it works.'

'But it will work.'

'All right. We'll try it.'

CHAPTER 2

The Tree of Mercury

David was reaching for a notepad. 'Now, we've got to be organized. We'll need sleeping-bags, matches, torch, penknife . . . '

'What for? I thought we were just going to warn the Prince and come back.'

'You never know,' David replied. 'Sometimes things happen that you don't expect. And then there's the alchemy. What are you supposed to mix the potion in?'

Charlotte had the alchemy book in her lap. 'It's called a crucible. It says, "a cauldron of sufficient bigness to stand in".' She looked up at her brother. 'Where are we going to get one of them? Couldn't we just use a normal cooking pot?'

'I expect we'd better do as it says,' said David. 'We'll try the junk shop. What else?'

'Bellows, a bucket, a length of rope . . . '

'Rope? What for?'

'It doesn't say.'

David frowned. 'That book doesn't give much away. What actually happens? And how's this world supposed to become real? Do you just suddenly end up there, or what?'

'I don't know.'

'Well, I wish we knew more about it.' David turned back to his list with a sigh. 'Also, we'll want woolly hats, thick socks, extra jumpers . . . '

'But it's the middle of May.'

'No it's not. In the book it's autumn.'

Charlotte stared. 'David, this is a bit frightening.'

'Do you still want to try it?'

Charlotte nodded.

'Then we'll look round at home for the bucket and rope, and go back to the junk shop for the other things. Have you got much money?'

'There's some left from my birthday. As long as cauldrons aren't too expensive . . . '

'And as long as he's got one to sell. Come on, then.' David tore his list out of the pad, while Charlotte went next door for her money. Then they ran downstairs, and David put his head inside the living room where their parents were watching television.

'We're just going out again,' he announced. 'Only to the junk shop—I mean across the park.'

'All right, David.'

They dashed out, and just heard Dad remark to Mum, 'I told you they'd find some new project. Children soon get over things.'

Back across the park they ran, between the sunbathers and footballers, dogs and kites, and back between the bollards to the junk shop. They burst into the shop, shattering its air of quiet decay.

'We'd like a cauldron, please,' said David, rather loudly, and the junkman looked up from his paper, startled.

'A cauldron?'

'Please say you've got one,' said Charlotte. 'It's got to be big enough to stand in.'

The junkman put down his paper and came out from behind the counter with a cough. 'Oh, I've *got* one, as it happens.' He shuffled over to a rusting pile of ironware, and began lifting off ancient horse harnesses, bits of weighing machines, and a dismembered firegrate.

Underneath sat a great iron pot, with a flared rim and a pair of lugs to lift it by, and a swelling, rounded body. It had a pair of iron feet, and leant rather lopsidedly on the ground. The children crowded round it; it came up to their knees, and certainly did look big enough to stand in.

'Genuine antique that,' said the junkman. 'Got a foot missing, of course: cost a bomb else. Fiver.'

'And . . . do you have any bellows?' asked David, taking his eyes away from the cauldron.

'Bellows! You're really kitting yourselves out, ain't you?' The junkman went to another part of the shop, and came back carrying what David had asked for. 'Leather's perished, but there's some puff in 'em if you squeeze hard. Tenner the lot, but since you're regulars so to speak, I'll do you 'em for eight quid. It's not part of your explosions, is it? I ain't heard no bangs yet.'

The children gave him a mysterious look, and Charlotte got out her purse. 'Eight pounds is all I've got left,' she whispered to David. 'I was saving it up.'

'I'll pay you back half,' said David, 'but it won't be for a while. Well? Do you still want to go ahead with it?'

Charlotte nodded, and held the money out to the junkman. Then they put the bellows in the cauldron and picked it up by its iron lugs. It swung uneasily between them, and David nearly knocked into one of the towers of junk.

'Easy there!' called the junkman. 'Can you manage? And don't play no dangerous games. I want to see you kids back again.'

The children made no reply, and staggered out of the shop with the cauldron between them. After they had gone some way down the street they dropped it with a clang.

14

'It weighs a ton!' Charlotte groaned. 'We'll never get it home.'

'You're right,' panted David. 'And I've been thinking: home's not the place. It's got to be secret. The book's right about that.'

'Well, what about the waste ground by the canal then? That's only just round the corner.'

'Right.'

They turned right, skirting the edge of the park, and moving in short runs with their arms stretched out for balance, dropping the cauldron when it got too heavy. At last they came to the railings, and the path that led between tall thickets of willowherb down to the canal.

'Hurry up!' Charlotte panted. 'Where are we going?'

'In here,' said David, and led them crashing off the path through the weeds. They let the cauldron drop and sat down to rub their hands and get their breaths back.

'Now we clear some of these weeds, so they don't catch fire.' David set to pulling up the tall stalks, and soon they had made a small clearing around the cauldron. The children stood and gazed at it solemnly. Standing alone among the broken willowherb stems the cauldron no longer looked like a piece of junk. Their thoughts ran back to the alchemy book, to the taming of spirits, and the mixing of potions with strange names: Orpiment, Shape-Changer, Little King.

'Come on,' said David after a while. 'We'd better get the rest of the things: we want to be done by teatime.'

They made their way quickly home and slipped upstairs, where they began digging through their cupboards and wardrobes. They got out their rucksacks, and the boots they took with them on walking holidays, and clothing was heaped together, sorted, and squashed into the smallest possible space. David was putting the alchemy bottles back in their box when Charlotte came in carrying her rucksack. She had a book in her hand, and David could see from the cover that it was *The Nine Sprites of the Tarn*.

'Good. We'll need that.'

Charlotte was leafing through the book, and then she looked up. 'I was thinking . . . you know you said sometimes unexpected things happen?'

David looked up and nodded.

'Well, why don't we tear the map out of the front of the book? So we can find our way around when we get there.'

David creased his forehead. 'I don't know . . . If we didn't put the map in along with the book, there might not be any places or scenery. Why not copy it out instead?'

Charlotte nodded, and set to work. David had meanwhile got the alchemy set packed up. He tried to cram it into the top of his rucksack. 'Charlotte?'

'Mm?'

'Can you take some of my clothes in your rucksack? That way I can carry the alchemy set.'

'All right . . . There: finished!'

Charlotte folded the map into her pocket, and they repacked their rucksacks. Then David made for the door. Charlotte hesitated.

'Well?'

'It's just . . . we don't really know what's going to happen, do we?'

'Maybe nothing, maybe lots,' replied David. 'Come on: it's time to give it a try.'

They crept downstairs as quietly as they could, but the kitchen door was open and Mum spotted them coming into the hall.

16

'You're not going out again, are you? What are you children up to?'

'Nothing, Mum,' said David, keeping his rucksack out of sight.

'Well, it's not long until tea.'

'Oh, we'll be back by then,' David promised. 'Come on, Charlotte.'

They escaped outdoors, and David led the way round the side of the house to the garage.

'What are we doing in here?' whispered Charlotte.

'Firewood. Here, can you manage an armful? And here's some newspaper and matches, too.'

'I've found a bucket, David. And isn't this Dad's tow rope?'

'Perfect. He won't mind: we'll put it back by tonight.'

David put the rope in the bucket and piled it full of firewood on top. Then they slipped across the street and along the edge of the park so as to keep out of sight from the house. 'It's only considerate,' David pointed out. 'If Mum and Dad saw us, they might be worried.'

'And there isn't any need,' Charlotte agreed.

The afternoon sun was slanting low across the canal when they threaded in among the willowherb and dropped their things beside the cauldron.

'Now, let's get a move on,' David said, and began building a fire using twigs and scrumpled-up newspaper. He laid larger sticks round it in a ring, and meanwhile Charlotte went off and came back with half a brick to prop the cauldron up where its foot was missing. They lowered the cauldron into place, and David struck a match. The light breeze blew it out, and it took several tries before the newspaper caught and the flames began to spread. Soon the old iron pot had a fire going under it, and David took the alchemy set out of his rucksack and reverently slid back the lid. Charlotte reached for the strange instruction book, and together they began to read.

'It starts with water,' said Charlotte. She took the bucket and fetched some from the canal, while David pored over the book, and began setting out the bottles and removing their stoppers, old withered corks that did not look as if they had budged in many long years.

'Quicksilver, Monk's Bane, Seed of Saturn, Salt of Wisdom . . . ' The water in the cauldron was beginning to steam, as David added the ingredients one by one, and each time the brew foamed up and then subsided into an oily, swirling mass.

'This is still the early part,' David explained, bending over the book. 'There's not too much danger yet.'

Charlotte stared. 'How do you mean, "danger"?'

'I don't quite know. Have a look.'

Charlotte took hold of the book. ' "Ye have planted the tree of Mercury," ' she read. ' "It remains that it be nourished, concocted, and digested with art. Let the fire be fed, and fanned well, until ye have a brew that glistens with perspicuity; but beware lest the heat fail: for then would your labour be lost, and all your gain be Death's Head." What does it mean? And what's Death's Head?'

'I don't know,' said David. 'Maybe we won't have to find out.' He stuffed some more logs under the cauldron, and got to work with the bellows. With each puff the logs glowed and then shot up in fresh flames. Soon the fire was roaring up round the sides of the cauldron, casting a reddish glow over the two alchemists.

'That's got it going!' he panted. 'How does it look now?'

18

But Charlotte was gazing speechless at the seething potion. It shifted its appearance moment by moment, taking on rich dyes, and tingeing the steam that came curling up from it with every colour of the rainbow. The liquid swirled and eddied, like a rocky pool beside a mountain stream, where the water comes hurrying in from the main current, churns round and round in a dark cauldron of rock, then finds its escape and roars out in a fresh series of falls.

'David—what's it doing?'

'Read the book! I mustn't stop!'

The bellows hummed and the fire growled round the cauldron, blackening its rusty old sides with a fresh layer of soot. Charlotte raised the book.

'"Our crucible is the world,"' she read, '"and in it all things are mirrored. It is tinctured with many colours, which come into being and pass away; spirit gives it life, and its body is Death's Head; and if life should fail, to Death's Head will it return."'

'What are you saying?' demanded David, on his knees beside the fire. 'I can't blow and think both at the same time!'

'I think,' began Charlotte slowly, gazing into the cauldron, 'it means that Death's Head is the stuff—the solid earth that's got to make the story real. By itself it's just dead, but if you add spirit, it can become absolutely anything—'

She broke off as the potion suddenly underwent a change. The colours faded, and now the cauldron seemed to be filled with liquid silver that rippled and shone like costly cloth. Bubbles rose and burst with a laugh or a murmur, or a snatch of words that Charlotte could not quite catch. She stared for a moment entranced, and then looked back to the book. The letters wound senselessly across the page in a maze of curls and flourishes. Then their meaning sprang out, and she stepped back from the cauldron.

'It's time to add the story.' She took *The Nine Sprites of the Tarn* out of her rucksack, and leafed through to the last chapter, where Prince Roland met his unhappy end. She took a firm hold of the pages and pulled. They came away in a bunch, and Charlotte folded them into her pocket. Then she reached out over the surface of the potion with the book in her hand. The fire glinted for a moment on the pale shapes of the Sprites on the cover, and then she let go, and the book slipped below the silvery ripples of their brew.

All at once, a light peal of laughter rose from the cauldron, along with a fresh train of bubbles, each bursting with a whisper. Steam floated up from the undulating surface of the liquid, and formed itself into fantastic shapes as it faded into the evening sky, now a woman's face, now a leaping dog, now a skull.

The fire was burning fiercely now, and David left his work to peer into the crucible. The flames lit their faces from below, while a silvery light shone from the potion, still seething and eddying like a stormy sea. At times a glassy calm spread over it, and then they glimpsed fragments of scenes: a wood, a house by a narrow bridge, a castle on a peak by the sea.

'What . . . what's happening?' whispered Charlotte.

'I don't know. What are we supposed to do next?'

Charlotte had hold of the book. 'Next we add the earth.'

'Earth?'

'Soil, gravel, ashes, stones: anything solid. Oh, David! Do we have to? It's so beautiful the way it is.'

Together they gazed into the sighing, rippling potion.

'Yes . . . but it isn't real. It's spirit without body. The two have to come together.'

'All right.' Charlotte tore herself away from the cauldron with a sigh, and began heaping earth and stones into the bucket using both hands, while David topped up the bucket and lifted it over the rim of the cauldron. As the first few stones pattered down into the liquid, the whispering grew fainter and the silvery light began to fade. At the same time the flames under the cauldron died away and the wood smoked and hissed as if water had been thrown on it.

'The bellows!' cried David. He crouched down and set to work. The wood glowed and smoke swirled around him. He pumped and pumped until at last fresh flames sprouted and began to leap round the cauldron.

'It's all right again,' called Charlotte, who was peering over the potion, now once more whispering and bubbling, flowing and ebbing and washing over itself. 'I'll put some more earth in: you keep blowing.' Then, to the droning of the bellows and the crackling of the fire, Charlotte little by little added more pebbles, earth, and stones, while the murmuring of the potion rose thicker all the time.

'David, it's working! It must be!' The fire was burning freely again, and David jumped up to join her. Charlotte lifted a large stone, and lowered it gently over the cauldron's rim. They stared at the rippling liquid as the stone sank, and the whispers rose as if in welcome. A moment later the whole silvery mass surged uneasily, the whispering died into silence, and up from the bottom welled a muddy belch of blackness that spread swiftly over the potion's surface. The fire hissed, the flames sank back, and clouds of smoke sprang from under the cauldron. David grabbed the bellows and crouched down to his work.

'Death's Head,' whispered Charlotte faintly. The smoke poured out thicker and thicker from the smouldering wood, and Charlotte slid extra kindling into the fire all round. Still David pumped at the bellows, and still the potion was black.

At last the flames began to revive, and Charlotte peered over the rim. In the midst of the blackness there was a faint thread of silver. It grew and branched, and in a few moments more the muddy stain had retreated to the edge of the cauldron and vanished. She heaved a sigh of relief, and then caught her breath.

'David, it's changing!'

'How do you mean?'

'I don't know, it's—' The silver was paling to white and then to blue, while the surging ripples grew fainter and fainter, until the cauldron looked like a well of still water reflecting the sky. Charlotte drew nearer and peered down, entranced. She reached out her hand to touch the water, which no longer looked at all hot, and found there was nothing to touch. Instead, a chill breeze blew past her fingers. She leaned over still further; now the blueness cleared, and she could see down, far down below the ground, below the canal, below the fire that burned under the cauldron. She saw treetops, and still further below she saw yellow leaves scattered on a forest floor. She drew back from the edge, feeling dizzy, while David got up and stood by her side.

'Is that . . . it?' she gasped.

David reached out his hand to the side of the cauldron. The fire was burning fiercely, sending choking streamers of hot smoke up past his face, but the iron was cold to the touch.

'That's your book,' confirmed David. 'Your world you wanted to go into. Well?'

Charlotte looked back at the cauldron. 'How do we get down?'

'That must be what the rope's for.'

'We'll never climb down all that way!'

'I'll tie some knots in it,' said David, picking up the coil. 'We'll be all right.' He set to work, while Charlotte turned her back. She had a sickening dread of climbing down inside the cauldron, with the fire underneath and all around, down where a moment before there had only been the seething, whispering potion. She shivered, and began gathering the bottles back into their box.

David meanwhile made the rope secure to one of the lugs of the cauldron, and dropped the rest of it inside. It brushed past the bare twigs and landed on the bed of leaves with a crackle. The children looked at each other.

'All right,' said David. 'I'll go first. And we'll take this with us too: you never know.' He slid the alchemy set into his rucksack and stepped up to the cauldron. Flames were shooting up all round its sides, and hot smoke swirled into his eyes. He paused for a moment, and then he jumped up to the rim and crouched there, with one hand on the rope and the other against the metal, the hole gaping below him and smoke blowing all around. Then he swung forwards, and his feet found the first of the knots. He lowered himself through the hole, and then he stuck fast. His rucksack was caught on the rim. He eased himself back up, and struggled his arms free one after the other; then, with his rucksack hooked over one arm across his chest, he began to climb down into the cauldron.

Charlotte watched from above as her brother swayed down the rope, lower and lower, past twigs and branches, until at last he landed with a rustle on the bed of leaves. She took a last look at her watch—five past six, late for tea—and then she gathered her courage, climbed up on the rim as David had done, and began to lower herself into the cold, bright air of an autumn day.

CHAPTER 3

Where Are We?

When Charlotte joined David at the foot of the rope she found herself standing on a soft bed of dead leaves, with a steel-blue sky above and empty forest all around. There was silence but for the occasional sigh of the wind, and the rattle of dry leaves being tumbled through the grass.

'Where are we?' said Charlotte, after they had gazed around in every direction.

'I'd say we're quite close to the Tarn,' said David. 'Oak and birch: the trees are right. And there isn't any other wood mentioned in the book.'

Charlotte's heart began to beat. 'Then the Prince should be nearby—and the Thing.'

David nodded. 'We'll explore. Quietly.'

They set off through the wood, skirting mossy boulders and crossing brilliant patches of yellow birch leaves. They looked carefully around as they went, and tried not to step on any twigs. After they had been wandering for some time, David nudged Charlotte's arm and pointed. Ahead there was a broad track running through the wood.

'Well?'

'Let's follow it,' said Charlotte.

The track led downhill, into a thicket which closed overhead to form a tunnel. Just beyond, where the sun fell bright and clear on the bronze of the leaf-strewn ground, they saw an old woman, bending down to pick up sticks. The children stopped.

'Who can it be?' Charlotte whispered. 'Mother Margery, the friendly old woman who spins?'

'It has to be,' said David. 'I don't think there are any other old women in the story.'

'And if it is her,' Charlotte went on, 'we really are close to the Tarn: she lives just below it. Let's go and talk to her.'

David nodded, and they set off down the track. As they came into the shadow of the bushes, the old woman looked up, then straightened slowly and stared at them with an expressionless face.

'We're strangers here—' David began.

'And kind ones,' the woman interrupted, 'I've no doubt. Won't you help an old woman in need? If you help me now, there's a chance I may help you later. That's fair, isn't it?'

'It must be her,' whispered Charlotte. 'Let's do what she says.'

David glanced up at the woman's face, gazing keenly into his. 'All right,' he whispered to his sister. 'It must be her—I suppose.' When he looked up again, the old woman was smiling. 'It sounds fair,' he said out loud. 'What would you like help with?'

The woman pointed to her bundle of sticks. 'I've such a hungry fire,' she complained. 'A poor woman can't feed it fast enough.'

So the three of them set about picking up sticks from along the track and the edges of the wood. Soon the old woman began to stray from the track, and David and Charlotte, who did not want to be left behind, followed her step by step into the wood.

'Where do you think she's leading us?' whispered David to Charlotte.

'We'll soon find out,' Charlotte whispered back. 'She said she'd help us.'

After a while, the children each had a sizeable bundle,

though the old woman hardly seemed to be carrying any more sticks than at the beginning. She straightened up again and looked round with an air of surprise. The track was nowhere in sight, and instead they found themselves in a thickly wooded valley, before the door of a cottage built of rough planks.

'Mercy, mercy me! You go to pick up sticks, and wander half across the forest! But we're home now, my dears, and you *will* just carry my sticks inside for me, won't you?'

The woman smiled, and David and Charlotte followed her into the house, wondering more and more.

'This isn't right,' Charlotte whispered as they crossed the threshold. 'Mother Margery doesn't live in the woods.' David cast her an anxious look, and then they were standing inside the old woman's house.

The room was neat, if rather bare. A cat slept on a chair by the fire, and the floorboards were swept clean by a broom that stood in a far corner. Otherwise, there was little to be seen; daylight glimmered in at the windows, but seemed unable to penetrate the shadows round the edges of the room, where large pieces of furniture were dimly visible in the light of the fire.

'In the corner, dears.' The old woman pointed to a large stack of firewood beside the roaring hearth. The children dropped their sticks on the pile, and then the old woman came forward with a bigger smile than ever.

'And now, my dears, seeing you've been so kind to me, I'd like to reward you. I'll give you three guesses!' She paused, holding her breath with a grin.

'You don't mean "three wishes"?' Charlotte hazarded.

'No, three guesses. And if you don't guess right, I'll eat you!' The old woman doubled up with a roar of laughter, as the children stared in horror. They turned to flee, but the door slammed shut, and the old woman's arms became claws that shot out after them. They dodged aside and edged round the room, darting their eyes this way and that for a means of escape.

'But what have we got to guess?' begged Charlotte.

'That's what I'm not telling you!' roared the witch, in fits of laughter. 'That's what you'll have to guess!' And she lunged at them again.

'Quick!' David shouted. They made for the dark corner where the broom stood, while the witch came trotting after them, chuckling with glee. The children sprinted across the floor, but the room seemed strangely distorted, and the distance was many times greater than it should have been. Just as they reached the corner, the old woman's voice sounded from behind.

'Broom, broom, sweep 'em up!'

The broom sat up on its bristles; it swayed and swelled, and grew to twice its size, and then it bore down on them, rasping the floor this way and that, while still the witch came chuckling and clumping along after them from behind.

'Up here!' shouted Charlotte, jumping up on to a brightly painted dresser, which had also grown to an outlandish size. Together, they struggled on to a high shelf running back towards the fire. Then they dashed on, dodging between jars and pots suddenly as big as themselves, which jumped into their way and rolled underfoot as if alive. Behind came the broom, sweeping all aside. The jars flew and rolled and broke, while the witch laughed louder than ever, hooting and pointing and clutching her sides.

'Charlotte,' David panted. 'The riddle—make a guess!'

'Is it . . . is it your age?' she gasped out.

'No!' roared the witch. 'It's not that! That's not what you have to guess!' She doubled up with another screech of mirth, and then she stopped laughing long enough to shriek out, 'Cat, cat, scratch 'em up!'

The tame, sleepy cat sprang from its chair with a snarl, and now it was a monster. It leapt up to the shelf, its yellow eyes flaming, and crouched in front of them, a tiger waiting to spring.

'Back down again!' David shouted, and they climbed hand over hand down a carved fretwork panel, past leering painted faces which followed them with their eyes. Charlotte jumped off with the broom sweeping and clattering after her, and the cat landed silently by David's side. They dodged behind the pile of sticks just ahead of their pursuers, while the witch came trotting up behind the cat and the broom, her snaggle-teeth bared in a grin.

'Is it,' David suggested, 'the number of teeth in your head?'

The old woman roared with laughter, and now they were backing into the fireplace, caught between cat, broom, and fire.

'No, no, oh my goodness!' moaned the witch, out of breath with chuckles. 'No, my dears, it isn't that! Fire, fire, *burn* 'em up!'

The fire sprang up with a roar, and the children just managed to jump aside as it shot out from the hearth, scorching a trail across the floor. Then the flames wheeled about and began to spread round them. David was knocked down by the broom, while the cat paced stealthily round in front of Charlotte to cut off her escape.

'A-hahaha! A-hahaha!'

The old woman was laughing and clapping her hands

as if it were the best show she had ever seen. Charlotte turned her eyes from the cat's yellow, mesmerizing stare and looked at the witch. For a moment everything seemed to stand still, and then she saw the solution to the riddle.

'Is it . . . the answer?'

'A—' The witch's cackle died as it was born, and a look of pure astonishment came over her face. Then she let out a tremendous howl of defeated rage. The fire gathered itself together, the broom stepped back, and the cat turned its maliceful glare in the old woman's direction. Then all three sprang at her. The witch screamed, as the three whirled round her in a blur. The fire burnt her up, the cat scratched her up, and the broom swept up what was left.

In a moment she was gone, and as David and Charlotte gaped at the space where she had been, the witch's three servants turned on the house. The fire ran along the shelves, scorching and kindling, and the cat slashed great rents in the plank walls with claws like scythes. Ash, dust, and debris flew about everywhere, and the broom followed behind sweeping it all away into nothingness, finishing up with the fire, the cat, and lastly itself. David and Charlotte were left sitting stunned on bare earth where a moment before there had been a house.

'Of course, "the answer" was the only answer possible,' said David, after they had sat in silence for a few moments. 'We had to guess what we had to guess, and she hadn't asked us to guess anything else. That was good thinking.'

'But who *was* she?' Charlotte burst out. 'There *aren't* any witches in the book! Are we in the wrong story, or what?'

'I don't know,' said David. 'Maybe. We'd better have a look at the map.'

Charlotte drew it out of her rucksack, and they scanned the landscape of the book, from the sea-cliffs of Beltenebros, up the Wandering Valley, and over the Heather Hills to the Tarn.

'Look!' said David, pointing to a spot near the coast. '"Old Woman's Cottage". Could that be it?'

'I suppose it *could*. But why put it on the map if it isn't in the story? And how did it come to life?'

'Well, we put the map into the cauldron along with everything else,' mused David. 'Maybe that was enough. It looks as if a whole world has come to life, and the story was only part of it. We're going to have to be very careful.'

'We certainly are!' retorted Charlotte. 'We were nearly *eaten*!'

'And just think: we let that witch trick us. It's not very good, considering we came here to save someone else from being tricked.'

'And look how far we are from the Tarn!' Charlotte went on. 'We only tore out the very last chapter. Oh, David, we're going to be too late! We'll never get there before the Prince is killed!'

'It's not just the time, either: it's the dangers,' frowned David. 'We might never get there at all.' He thought a moment, and then pointed to the map. 'Look, we may be a long way from the Tarn, but we're not far from Beltenebros. That's where the King lives. What if we took him word? Warned him?'

'And he could send someone,' Charlotte agreed. 'Knights or soldiers. They'd get there safe, and travel quicker than we could.'

'That's if he believes us,' David pointed out.

'Why shouldn't he?'

'Well, people don't always.'

'He'll have to when we show him these.' Charlotte pulled out the pages she had torn from the book before they left. David smiled.

'All right, let's go. I just hope we're right about where we are. This valley *ought* to lead us to the coast.'

'Well, why don't we find out?'

They jumped to their feet, shouldered their rucksacks, and set off. Rocky walls rose up steeply on either side, and the valley bottom was boggy and overgrown. Thickets of willow and alder blocked their way, and in places they had to scramble down faces of rock where the sluggish stream pattered down as a trickling waterfall. The afternoon wore away, and the sun was slanting redly through the trees when they felt a keen breeze in their faces. Then the wood suddenly came to an end, and they found themselves standing on the edge of a cliff.

Ahead lay the sea, a misty turquoise in the evening light. Its face was dotted with fishing smacks, which had hoisted their brown sails and were putting back in to port for the night. Some way to their left the cliffs sloped down to a sheltered cove, where a river flowed into the sea. A town huddled there, and beyond it rose a great crag with a castle on top, proud and bright in the setting sun.

'That's it!' said David. 'Beltenebros.'

CHAPTER 4

Beltenebros

'Let's hurry,' said David. 'We want to be sure we see the King tonight.'

They careered down the grassy slope, ran over the bridge across the river, and came into the town just as the sun was setting behind the hills in the West. The last of the fishing-smacks had put in, and the small harbour was thronged with people. Some were hanging up nets, while others unloaded lobster pots and baskets of fish and crabs, or drew their boats up on to dry land for the night. The children wandered among the crowd, and wherever they went they were met by stares. They asked several of the fishermen if they knew how they could get to see the King, but for reply they were stared at wider than ever, and those nearby moved off, muttering and shaking their heads.

'Do you think it's our clothes?' David whispered, as they turned up a street leading away from the sea, and came upon a knot of staring women, in bright dresses and white bonnets.

'We're the ones who ought to be staring at *them*, if so,' replied Charlotte. 'Why are they all so silent?'

They walked on, through narrow streets paved with rough cobbles and earth, and sometimes up flights of steps where the town began to climb the hillside. Then they came to a square and found a group of boys of about their own age lounging on the steps of a fountain. They were dressed in a kind of uniform, with green pleated jackets and trailing sleeves, and they were playing at dice.

'Seven again!' one of them shouted. 'I'll win your jerkin from you before nightfall, Peregrine, and you'll be whipped by the steward.'

''Tis well known that Oliver has a pact with a spirit,' remarked one of the others, as Peregrine handed over some copper coins to the boy who had spoken first. 'It serves him now for seven years, but then it will come in a whirlwind and carry him off.'

'Do not jest with such matters,' Oliver retorted. 'If the King heard you speak thus, his melancholy fit would come again.'

At this moment, David and Charlotte approached the group.

'Excuse me,' began David, and all the faces turned to stare. 'Do you know how we could get to see the King? It's very important.'

The stares went on, and then the one who was called Peregrine spoke. 'Do you not know? The King sees no one.'

'Why not?' demanded Charlotte.

'Out of grief,' stated Peregrine, while the other boys exchanged looks of wonder at the strangers' ignorance. 'Grief for his ward, the Princess Melisande, stolen away by—something I dare not name, on the very day she was to have wedded his son, Prince Roland. And that same morn the Prince too departed, to travel to the West and save his betrothed.'

'None doubts the Prince's valour,' put in Oliver, 'but he is young and untried in any fight. He went alone, and the King despairs of his return.'

'And so King Stephen sits in his tower and grieves, and will see no one,' concluded Peregrine.

Charlotte and David exchanged glances.

'When did Prince Roland leave?' asked David.

'Two days since.'

'Then he's not dead yet!' burst out Charlotte with relief. The boys leapt to their feet.

'How say you?' demanded Peregrine. 'What know you of the Prince?'

'Aye, and whence come you, with your outlandish speech and garments?' asked one of the others.

'You're the ones who talk funny,' retorted Charlotte, while David nudged her in the ribs.

'We've got to see the King,' David repeated. 'It's the only way of saving the Prince's life. You talked about seeing him yourselves, just before we came.'

'Aye, we are his pages. We see him right enough.'

'Though 'tis seldom he sees us,' added Oliver. 'His moods and his melancholy make him blind.'

'Well, if he can't see us, at least he can hear us,' said Charlotte. 'He's got to!'

'We know what's going to happen,' said David. 'We have a book that can't be wrong—unless you *make* it wrong. And we're the only ones who can.'

Peregrine eyed them shrewdly. 'Are you wizards?'

'We're alchemists,' answered David. 'And we've come here from another world.'

'So you say. You must be wizards indeed if you seek to tame King Stephen when the fit is on him. He is troubled by dreams, and fancies some omen of misfortune in all he sees or hears. At times he rages and rails for an hour together, if someone has spoken a word amiss, and put him in mind of his grief. Then he will dash his crown to the floor and tear his hair, and curse all who come near with terrible, biting oaths.

'But go,' Peregrine continued, folding his arms with a smile. 'Do with him as you say. 'Twould be a rare jest to see such wizards as these tell King Stephen to his face that his son must die, would it not, lads?'

'Aye, when he boggles at a flight of crows,' said one.

'Or if we cross his chamber in thirteen steps, or ladle soup with the left hand.'

'Go, do as you say,' went on Peregrine. 'I shall follow after, pull his beard and steal his crown. I warrant he shall be angrier with you than with me!'

'It doesn't make any difference,' said Charlotte. 'We've still got to see him.'

'Can't you smuggle us in?' David argued. 'Disguise us?'

Peregrine turned to his friends. 'What say you, lads? Shall we do it for the jest's sake? Guy and Walter, you are something near our wizards' sizes. Make an exchange of your garments, and we shall see how witchcraft and eloquence can fare against an old man's melancholy.'

'You'll really help us?' gasped Charlotte.

'For the jest's sake, aye,' said Peregrine with a twinkle in his eye. 'Whether there be truth in your tale I know not: I hope there is none, for the King will never listen, and the Prince will assuredly die. Come, my lads, pack up your dice. The hour of the King's dinner approaches: we have tarried too long, and the steward will chide us.'

The pages scrambled to their feet and sped off to the Castle, while Peregrine, Guy, and Walter led David and Charlotte to a nearby stable. There they exchanged clothes, hid their rucksacks in some straw, and left the two disconsolate-looking pages to guard them.

'Attend to what I say,' Peregrine warned them, as they followed him up the winding road that led to the castle on the peak, now clad in odd-feeling jerkins and hose.

'You are to wait on the King as he dines. You must kneel as you offer the King his cup, and bow thrice as you take it away. Walk ever slowly, for the King detests haste; and be not tardy, for he cannot brook delays. Look humble, and speak soft, and have a care for his moods.'

'We'll try,' Charlotte promised, 'but he's going to get a nasty shock at some point in his meal.'

'A true word,' observed Peregrine with a wry look, and they continued on their way in silence.

Up and up the track ran, until at last it levelled out before the mighty barbican. Torches blazed over the gateway in the evening air, and guards were posted on either side, mail-clad, with halberds in their hands. The children bent their heads down, trusting to the darkness, and hurried past, over the drawbridge and across a glaring, smoky courtyard, where men-at-arms were being marshalled into watches.

From there, Peregrine led them through the dark void of the Great Hall. It was still decked out for the wedding feast with banners and streamers, which now hung mournfully in the gloom, while shrivelling wreaths of late roses cast their stale, sweet scent over the air. From that cold and lonely place they passed to a gaping cavern of a room, alive with bustle and warmth, and lit like a scene from the inferno by three mighty fires. Sides of sheep and oxen were roasting slowly by the hearths, while a flickering light played on the faces of cooks and scullions, sending monstrous shadows dancing up the walls.

The smell made David and Charlotte remember their hours without eating, but before they could say anything to Peregrine, they were startled by an angry shout from behind.

'Miscreants!' roared a voice, and a stout figure came forward carrying a long staff.

''Tis the steward,' Peregrine whispered, and then executed a deep and respectful bow.

'Aye, well enough to bow, after dicing the day away. Make haste! The King has the black mood on him.'

They picked up a dish each and followed Peregrine up a long and dizzying stair. At last they emerged in a dark, vaulted hall at the top of the tower. This was King Stephen's retreat, and here he sat over his meals with none for company but his chamberlain, the Wizard Mortagon.

'Come,' whispered their guide, and the children approached the King's table with their hearts in their mouths. At the centre of the table sat the King, with burning eyes and a sad mouth over a grizzled chin. He wore a mantle of fur against the cold of the room, and a circle of gold rested in his whitening hair. On his left stood the great ceremonial salt, and below should have been his retainers; but there were none. To his right sat the wizard, his eyes playing constantly about the room, while the King's stared always fixedly in front.

'What now?' whispered Charlotte.

'Wait till the meal's over, if he's in a bad mood,' David replied, and then Peregrine hurried them forward to the table.

The meal had its tricky moments. When Charlotte was told to help the King wash his hands, she became entangled in basins, ewers, and towels, and was only saved by Peregrine, who mimed what she had to do behind the King's chair. Then David was asked to carve the partridges, and a crisis came.

'Nay, page, page,' the King protested, wakening at last from his stupor, 'how will there be meat left to eat if you hack it so? Nay, take it away, I will have more wine instead. Nay, take the wine away: it saps my strength. I will have Melisande to come and sing for me . . . but she is gone. Nay, page! What page are you? Are you a page or not a page?'

David was caught with the platter in his hand, and set it down again slowly. 'I'm not a page,' he said, looking first to the King and then the wizard, who was gazing on him keenly. 'We had to see you, and it was the only way. It's your son: he's in danger.'

The King looked up, his eyes flaming, red and troubled. His voice sounded low and choked. 'What is this?'

'Prince Roland,' put in Charlotte, coming forward. 'We know all about his quest, and if you don't send someone after him, he'll be killed!'

The King's jaw fell in angry amazement, while the wizard was staring hard, not unkindly, but as if he were trying to see right into the children, and judge whether they spoke with truth or falsehood. Then the King staggered from his chair. 'Thunder and fire! Will I ever be plagued with nightmares? Omens of evil, pages that are prophets, birds that fly in nines, right to left, and caw out my doom! What are you? Are you spirits?'

'No,' said David, taking a pace back. 'But we *have* come from another world. That's how we know.'

Now Mortagon spoke. He licked his narrow lips, and lifted a bony hand from his dark robe. He pointed it at the children, as if casting a spell on them to make them speak. 'What world, and how did ye come?'

'We call it the real world,' Charlotte replied carefully. 'At least, people there think it's realer than this. And we came by alchemy.'

Mortagon nodded slowly, while the King sank back into his chair, shuddering after his outburst.

'Say on,' commanded Mortagon gravely, and David felt that the wizard would weigh his words fairly: but he must make every word count.

'It's been written what will happen to Prince Roland,' said David. 'We have the writing here. It was written in our world about yours, and that means it can't be wrong.'

'It's like fate,' said Charlotte. 'But you can change it: you must! He'll be drowned!'

There was silence, while the wizard went on looking at them from under his dark brows, and the King slowly lifted his head. 'Mortagon,' he murmured. 'Counsel us. What are they?'

'Sire, I know not,' replied the wizard. 'Spirits, as I imagine, from a purer realm, but whether lying or true, I know not. There be hidden things, sire, books of secrets, and very worlds and oceans of truth, of which we know naught. But likewise are there illusions, false seemings, and Sprites that delight in trickery.'

'But that's just it,' Charlotte almost sobbed. '*We're* not out to trick you! It's the Sprite of the Tarn: she'll promise him things, and he'll believe her. And then she'll kill him! The flesh will be eaten off his bones! See! Read it!'

She threw the loose pages down on the table in front of the King, and his horror-struck eye travelled over the closing words of the book. His voice choked in his throat, his knuckles whitened on the arms of his chair, and then he stared at the two false pages with a face of agony.

'Nay,' he mumbled. 'My son will judge the true from the false. He carries a sword of bite . . . and is pure of heart . . . he will judge rightly.'

'How can he?' demanded David severely. 'You can't

fight lies with a sword. What chance will he have, alone? And we *know* what will happen. Send someone. Warn him. You must!'

The King raised his eyes from the paper. 'Nay,' he said slowly. 'Prophets, oracles, omens . . . oft the stars portend one thing, and another comes about. Prophets lie, omens are false; we live in a world of dreams, and the future is dark. Take your book of oracles.' He nudged the pile of papers in their direction. 'I am old, and live for the day. There are no Sprites, and you are no prophets. I mistook you, and I am sorry for it. I see now: you are Walter, and Guy, are you not? An old man forgets his servants' faces. Go now, go. I am tired. Mortagon, you will mix me a sleeping-draught tonight, one to banish dreams. Enough of talk.'

He rose from his chair, swaying and shaking his head, and looking down to avoid the children's eyes. They stood and stared in disbelief, while the King shuffled out of the room. Mortagon got up to follow, and turned at the door to give them a last searching look. He seemed to waver, but then came a sharp word from the King, and the wizard's face vanished into the darkness.

The children stood dumb, while a breeze ruffled the papers on the table.

'He nearly believed us—so nearly!' Charlotte swallowed to stop herself from crying. 'David, he'll be drowned!'

David reached forward and picked up the pages. The last one was on top.

'We'll go there,' he said. 'We'll go to the Tarn and save him ourselves.'

CHAPTER 5

The Hounds of the Hills

Later that night, David and Charlotte were sitting in the straw of their stable, finishing a late supper of scraps from the King's table given to them by the pages. The map was spread out between them.

'The Wandering Valley runs all the way from Beltenebros to the Tarn,' David was saying, 'but it's two days' walk.'

'That's too long!' Charlotte objected. 'In two days he'll be dead! He's there now. The Sprites could get him at any time!'

'And that's not the only problem. Halfway up the valley there's the Giant.' David's finger pointed to a spot marked 'Castle of the Giant Rodomont'. 'Prince Roland got past all right in the story, but *we* might not.'

'I'm not tangling with any giant,' Charlotte declared. 'They're bound to eat children, if witches do. Look, why don't we go up the valley a little way and then take a short cut across? It doesn't look like hard going: the road only runs out right at the end where you come to the Heather Hills. We might save a day.' She looked at David eagerly, but he was frowning.

'But then there's just one problem.' And he pointed to the words 'Hounds of the Hills', which stretched across the map, the full length of the Heather Hills.

'Well, they're not in the book,' Charlotte pointed out. 'They might not even exist, or they mightn't be anything too bad.'

'The witch existed,' said David. 'They're likely to be something pretty nasty, if you ask me.'

'But we *know* the giant is, and if we don't risk it we're going to be too late. Come on, David! We've got to!'

'Then there's something else. How long are we planning to be away? It's been hours already. Mum and Dad are going to be worried sick.'

'You said things in books don't take up real time.'

'But we don't really know. And we're not exactly in a book, are we? We made it real.'

'Well, if we don't do something the Prince'll be *dead*, and that's heaps worse than just being worried. Come on, we've got to. It's a short cut: we'll be as quick as we can.'

David heaved a sigh. 'All right. The Hounds it is.' He folded the map with a huge yawn. 'Now let's sleep: it must be nearly morning, in proper time.'

They settled down in the straw, and before they even knew they were asleep it was day, and Peregrine had appeared with a basket of food.

'Fresh bread, cold fowl, butter, and cheese . . . I fear 'tis all the help we can offer you. And now you must go, far and fast, for the King's wits are wandering. He speaks of spirits and demons, and would have the town searched for spies.'

The children struggled up from the straw, thanking him and rubbing the sleep from their eyes. Peregrine meanwhile eyed them dolefully. 'Did I not warn you how 'twould be? And whither now would you flee?'

'To the Tarn to find the Prince, of course,' said Charlotte, before David could stop her. Peregrine's eyes opened wide.

'Another merry jest, to be sure, with all the beasts and boggarts of the wilds on your heels. Yet to finish up in the pot after all is poor sport.'

'No one's putting us in the pot,' said David confidently. 'Thanks for your help.'

'Nay, cooked or raw, 'tis all one,' replied Peregrine, pressing the basket into Charlotte's hands. 'Now begone. Good fortune and good speed!'

The children shouldered their rucksacks and set off quickly through the streets, with a last troubled wave from Peregrine. The early morning sun cast long shadows in front of them; already the fishermen were running their boats down to the sea. David and Charlotte hurried along, looking out for men-at-arms come in search of them. They followed the river upstream, and soon they came to the edge of the town. Ahead, a broad highroad stretched off up the valley, rising and dipping and finally disappearing from view in a fold in the hills. Patches of larch and oak glowed orange against the green of the pastures, and flocks of sheep drifted across the distant hillsides like gulls wheeling far out over the sea.

'Well, there's no bus,' said David, 'so let's walk.' The cold air encouraged a brisk pace, and by mid-morning they came to a crossroads. Here they left the main road, and branched off to the right up the valley side. Soon the Wandering Valley lay behind, and a rolling, wooded countryside stretched ahead, with purple-brown hills away in the distance.

All day they walked, through dense woods and open pastures, straggling villages and sleepy towns. They ate their lunch looking back on the sea, a glittering blue line far off to the east. Soon after that the road began to wind and climb. Bracken-clad slopes rose on either side, and then the road turned into a broken track, and began twisting its way up a stony ravine. By the time they came out at the head of the ravine they were just in time to see the last of the sun, sinking into a murky bank of cloud low over the horizon. Ahead of them lay bare, rounded folds of brown and blue: the Heather Hills.

'Come on, then,' said David. 'Not far now: just over that brow should be the Wandering Valley.'

They set off briskly along the narrow path through the bracken, and then they saw a surge of movement up ahead. As it came closer, they realized it was a herdsman, driving his sheep before him. In a moment the sheep were milling round them, and the herdsman stared at them with wide eyes.

'What is it?' Charlotte demanded, but the man only stared, and then pointed at the sun and lowered his arm as if to show it setting. Then he shook his head, still staring at them, and made a noise like the barking of a dog.

'What do you mean?' asked David, but he was gone, driving his sheep down off the hills, and turning every few paces to stare back and shake his head.

'A bit simple in the head, maybe,' ventured Charlotte, but both were thinking of the Hounds, and after that they said nothing.

Dusk crept quickly over the hills, and the air grew cold. Ahead, the evening star shone in place of the sun in a glowing, pale green sky; but the landscape around them was darkening, and deep shadows had gathered in the rocky hollows and under the clumps of heather and bracken. The children quickened their pace. Then David started at a sudden sound.

'What was that?'

'A stray sheep?'

'Possibly . . . ' David was peering off to one side, where there was a ruffled motion through the bracken, like a breath of wind that stirred there and nowhere else.

45

'There!' shouted Charlotte, and pointed to a clump of heather. 'I saw a face! I'm sure I did!'

But whatever it was, the shadows had closed over it. The children hurried on, and now whispers rose around them, and they could hear the drumming of feet on the path behind. David looked round.

'Charlotte, we're being chased!'

She looked back, and saw a stream of pale shapes bounding along the twisting path after them. Other shapes rustled through the bracken on either side, or leapt from bush to bush further off, running parallel and hemming them in. Now the whispers rose up from all round, louder and clearer than before.

'Hark! Hist!'

'Sniff the scent!'

'Track them! Track them!'

'Hunt them down!'

They were running at full pelt now, stumbling over the tough roots of the heather and jumping round stones, while the feet of the Hounds pounded after them behind.

'Seek them, find them, catch them, caught!'

With the last words, a large shape jumped out on to the path right in front of them, and they skidded to a halt. It was the size of a man, and as lithe as a cat, with tawny skin like a lion's. But what appalled them was its face. Human eyes, deep with cunning, stared out from below a dog's ears, and human lips stretched round its twitching muzzle and curved up in a hideous smile. Its eyes flickered between them, and then it spoke.

'Riddle me this: where will you flee?'

They glanced back, and the Hounds were almost on them, when the beast in front leapt aside and pranced round them, as if enjoying the sport. They set off again at the run.

'David! We've got to do something!'

'Try the food!' David panted, as they sprang over whole bends in the path, their eyes fixed on the darkening hillside that still rose higher ahead. Charlotte reached into the basket and flicked out the cloth that covered their food.

'A rag! A wipe! We want to be fed!' the voices chanted, and now Charlotte's hand lit on a clutch of boiled eggs, which she flung out behind as they flew wildly on. She glanced back, and almost wept to see the Hounds pause in their chase, and go sniffing round the eggs.

'An egg! An egg!'

'The fruit of the fowl!'

They ran on, leaving the Hounds a good way behind. But the eggs were soon gone, and now the Hounds came streaming after them along the path, setting up a baying that echoed round the empty hills.

'And now the feast!'

'Seek them, find them, catch them, caught!'

'The chicken, Charlotte!' David gasped, and Charlotte tossed out what was left of the fowl Peregrine had given them.

Again the Hounds paused, and for a minute or two the sounds of their champing and snaffling grew fainter behind.

'We're nearly to the top,' panted Charlotte. 'If only . . . they don't . . . come after us again! I can't run—'

She turned to look back, just as the baying began again, and the Hounds of the Hills came bounding on.

'We've had our fowl: now give us meat!'

'Blood to drink, and flesh to eat!'

'There *is* none,' wailed Charlotte, and 'Only us,' added David. Their breath was giving out, their sides were aching and their feet stumbled, but they had come to the crest of the hill at last, and below they saw all the valley spread out in the deepening dusk. Black hills rose against an ultramarine sky, while down in the valley bottom there shone the lights of a village. The land dropped away almost sheer, and the path turned to slant gently down to the bottom in a series of long zigzags.

'We're done with play, we've had our sport!'

'Seek them, find them, catch them, caught!'

'Come on!' panted David, and sprinted down the path.

'No!' Charlotte ran behind, trying to speak between gasps for breath. 'This time . . . they mean it. No good . . . on path.'

David glanced back. The gap between the Hounds and their prey was closing rapidly. Charlotte looked over the edge of the path down the slope, and then back at the Hounds. Then she flung their food basket behind her and jumped. David came after her, and together they went rolling, skidding, and tumbling down the broken hillside, their packs jarring round their ears, dodging rocks and thorn-bushes, running and falling and running again.

The Hounds swerved from the path in fury, and came careering down the hill after them. But they had no advantage on such steep ground. Soon the children could hear yells and howls from behind, and the sound of heavy bodies crashing through bracken and thudding against the hard earth. On and on they rolled in the near-darkness, and always the snarls and curses of the Hounds sounded in their ears.

'Bite them, crush them, gnaw and slay!'

'Fools we were! Too long at play!'

48

The glimmering lights of the village shone nearer now, but the slope was levelling out, and once they were on the flat the Hounds would soon catch up.

'Last . . . dash,' panted Charlotte, and together they threw themselves into a sprint. Some way ahead they could see the first house of the village. Nearer and nearer they came to the light; but the Hounds were racing after them on the flat, and their baying rose up like the roar of a gale. Now they could see a lighted window and an open door. A figure was standing on the step. It was an old woman, and in her hand she held something white. First David, then Charlotte came skidding up to the doorway.

'Make a mark on the post!'

The children hung back, remembering the witch. But the Hounds were springing out of the dark into the circle of light that shone from the house, and the face before them was kindly and urgent.

'Quick! Mark the post with the chalk: 'twill keep you from harm.'

The wooden doorpost had a white cross drawn on it with a line underneath. David drew another line below it, and Charlotte did the same. Then they tumbled inside, the door slammed, and a creature thudded against it and recoiled with a howl of fear and rage.

CHAPTER 6

A Tale of Here and Now

David and Charlotte sank to the ground, sobbing and panting for breath. Outside they could hear the Hounds of the Hills howling round and round the house, pacing heavily on the dry earth, and sniffing about for some chink in the old woman's magic.

'They cannot pass,' said the woman. 'A rowan post is a sure charm against witchery. There now, all's as safe as safe. Come by the fire, and think no more of evil things.'

The old woman led them in front of the roaring blaze which gave the room its only light, sat them on stools, and wrapped them in blankets, still shuddering and staring with shock. Little by little the warmth and safety of the charmed house revived them. The woman moved silently about the room, and in a few minutes handed them bowls of hot porridge. The baying of the Hounds was growing fainter now. The porridge settled in their stomachs, comforting and warm, and they found themselves staring into the fire, letting its changing forms and landscapes steal through their minds. The old woman sat back in a worn chair with a plain wooden seat and panelled back, and nodded with approval.

'There's little evil can visit an honest hearth,' she said. 'The Hounds will tire soon and slink back to their dens.' She took a long clay pipe down from a shelf and lit it from the fire, then went for a basket of carded wool and sat down to spin. Soon the whirring of the wheel and gentle crackle and hiss of the fire sent the children into a doze.

After a time, something roused them. It was a knock
on the door. The old woman was holding it open, while
on the threshold stood a newcomer. It was a younger
woman, with a spinning wheel under one arm and a
basket of wool on the other. In her hand she held a piece
of chalk, and added another line to the three already on
the rowan post.

'Why, Winifred,' said their hostess. 'Make your mark
well, for the Hounds have been out. Now come in by
the fire and take a stool.'

'I thank you, Mother Margery.'

The young woman smiled at the children, and sat
beside them with her wheel in front of her. While she
was reaching for some wool, there was another knock,
and three more women were let in. Each carried a
spinning wheel, and each made her mark on the post
before coming in and taking a seat by the fire.

The flames seemed to leap up in welcome, and the
children gazed in wonder at the circle of wheels now
ranged round the fire, with the women's faces, young
and old, glimmering in the uncertain, changing light.
Each reached into her basket for some wool, and soon
the spinning wheels were humming in concert. Mother
Margery puffed at her pipe and sat down once again to
her wheel, winding off the thread and fixing a fresh
spindle with deft hands. Her wheel was larger and older
than the others; carved words and signs ran round its
rim, and flowed together into motion as she set to her
work.

David and Charlotte sank into a kind of trance, as if
in a dream where there were no thoughts, only a
mingling of sounds and sights, shadows and dancing
light, the roar of the fire up the flue and a last howl that
drifted down from the hills, and over all the rhythmical

whirr of the spinning wheels. Louder and softer it came, like a chorus of crickets in summer, when the hay is mown and the meadows are parched, and there is time at last to bask in the sun and dream.

After the women had been spinning for some time, Mother Margery knocked out her pipe and spoke.

'Well now, my dears, what tale will you have? Will it be a tale of long ago and far away, or a tale of here and now?'

'Let it be a tale of here and now, if you please,' said one of the younger women, and the others nodded. 'Aye, Mother, here and now.'

Mother Margery leant back and gazed into the darkness, while her fingers went on with their task. 'Here and now, here and now. Well then, the world is wide, my dears, and time is long; but there is wonder enough in the here and the now.

'Beside my door there runs a stream, and over the stream there is a bridge; and if you crossed that bridge, you would find a path that winds up and winds around, and crosses the meadows and comes to a stile. That's where the woods begin, dense old hollies, planted there before ever men came to this valley. But the path goes on, and in a little time you would come to a place of rocks and hills and ancient oaks, and in the midst of these there is a Tarn.'

The children started, and looked up from the fire. The women were nodding: they knew the place.

'The moon has risen, my dears,' the old woman went on. 'You might find your way there even now, if you wished.' She paused, and the youngest of the women shuddered.

'Oh, no, Mother, not I, not by night, and not by moonshine, least of all.'

Mother Margery smiled. 'It is an uncanny place enough, whether on a winter's night or a summer's day. Its face is a mirror, calm and fair: 'tis never stirred or troubled, not by wind nor rain nor frost, nor by the falling leaves of autumn. Nine streams feed it, and nine Sprites dwell in it; and they are very lovely to look upon, as they dance over the water on a moonlit night. But you must be wary if you would spy on their revels, for there are those who go and never return.

'Aye,' she went on, nodding gently. 'The Sprites are fair, and fair and bright is the Tarn to look upon. But 'tis the same as with some folk that are fair and smiling of face, but in their hearts is naught but scheming and malice; or an apple, sweet-smelling without, but rotten within, where a worm gnaws at its core. Just so is the Tarn, for though it be clear and still above, deep below 'tis all mud and bones, raging and churning round and round without cease.'

She paused; the spinning wheels whirred on, the flames crackled and leapt, and the women were hushed and tense with expectation. David and Charlotte felt chilled despite the warmth of the fire. Their eyes were fixed on Mother Margery, who gazed straight ahead into the darkness, and then resumed her tale.

'Aye, deep below its waters rage and churn, and the bones of those that are drowned have no rest. There is a stair that winds down and down to the very bottom; for the sides of the Tarn are sheer. And up this stair on certain nights come the ghosts of the drowned, when their restlessness grows too strong. They flit along the stair, and their steps never wear the stone, for all the thousands of times they come and go.'

Once more she paused, and Charlotte managed to whisper, 'What do they do?'

'They flock to the places they knew in life. You have all seen them,' went on Mother Margery, looking round the circle of nodding women. 'They look in at windows, or dog the steps of those they loved. Some hang back and will not be seen, and others rage and rave like a gale through the streets. They whistle in the eaves and rattle the doors; but for all their roaming and flitting they can do naught for good or ill, for the ghosts of the dead are as empty as air.'

'One followed me here,' remarked the youngest of the women. ''Twas Jenny. I saw her alive not seven days since. She told me she would go in search of her sweetheart that was drowned, and now I believe she has gone to him in the Tarn. She followed me close, pale and silent, then broke away when I came nigh to the witch-post. A wild, crazed thing she was, fleeing back up into the woods where now she must dwell.'

The others began to murmur, and Mother Margery nodded slowly. 'Aye, Jenny was the wildest in life, and would be wildest in death.' She fell silent, and the children exchanged frightened looks. This was the fate that awaited Prince Roland if they failed: not just death, but death without rest, endlessly trudging the long, winding stair, back to the scenes he knew in life, then down once more to the churning waters of the Tarn, a ghost whose bones could never sleep. They were shaken from their thoughts by the old woman's voice.

'No, my dears, their bones will never rest until the storm beneath the waters ceases to blow, and that will never happen until the Thing that dwells below is slain.'

'And when will that be, Mother?' asked one of the women.

'Soon, my dears, soon. For Prince Roland has come,

and he will sweep the Worm away. Now listen, and I will tell you the tale. Under the Tarn the storm never rests; but at the eye of the storm there is a house, and in it dwells the Thing. Folk give it many names, and that is a sign how much they fear it. 'Tis called the Worm, the Fish with many legs, the Deceiver, and other names besides. None of you have seen it, I'll wager, for it keeps mostly to its den; but there are rare times when it swims up from below and crawls to land, and steals off through the forest in search of harm.

'Now, last year King Stephen went to visit his brother, who reigns over a neighbouring kingdom away beyond the hills. It was midwinter when he returned, and came riding through the woods just up the valley from here. Now that is a fickle time, my dears. The paths no longer run straight, but turn back on themselves just as they would have led a traveller safe from the wilds. For long the King and his party wandered in the snowy woods, and then they came to what looked like a wall of chain mail, glittering in the sun. They followed it round, and they followed it round, and then the King knew he was hemmed in every way. It was the Worm that had him in its coils, and then it rested its great head on its body, and stared at him with yellow eyes.

'Now King Stephen is old, but he would have drawn his sword none the less and made to fight it, had it not been for a look in the Thing's eye that was near human, and made him pause. So he waited, and then it spoke.

' "You are lost, King Stephen," it said; and these are its very words, as the Prince himself told them to me. "You are lost," it said. "These woods are a maze, and the paths will betray you, if you have no guide. But where will you find one, King Stephen? And how will you pay his wage?"

'Now at this, King Stephen drew his sword, and the Thing tensed all along its body, with a sound like the clashing of armour. It raised its head over him, and then it sank down again on its coils. "Nay," it said, speaking soft and low, "be not angry. I shall be your guide."

'"And your payment?" asked the King, for he was wary, and close on as cunning as the dragon.

'"Naught but the first living thing you see when you come safe back to your town. Small payment enough, I think, for saving a king."

'The King thought hard, for he mistrusted the beast, and feared to bargain with it. But he had sent no word of his homecoming, and so no crowd would meet him when he returned; the first creature he saw was like to be some stray dog or fowl on the edge of the town, and no ill would come of its loss.

'So he agreed. The creature smiled all along its scaly face, and its tongue licked out like a flame. Then its coils began to unwind, layer on layer, and soon the King was free. The Thing bade him follow, and as it slid off through the trees over the fresh snow the paths straightened, and soon they came to the edge of the wood.

'"Remember your bargain," the Thing warned him. "You will forget, but I shall come and remind you of it at the right time." With that, it turned its yellow eyes from the King, and its head curled back into the trees and was gone.

'The King was in good spirits after this, well pleased to have escaped from the woods, and his pact with the dragon was soon far from his mind. He never thought of it, even when he came riding down the Wandering Valley to the sea, where stands Beltenebros. But just as he came to the town, and was riding between the first of the houses, the Princess Melisande ran out to meet him. She had watched for him every day, and had seen him coming from afar off.

'King Stephen trembled, but said naught, and feigned to smile. Time passed; the Thing never came, and the King lost his fear. He spoke lightly of his bargain, thinking he had cheated the Thing of its due, and his courtiers praised him for his cunning.

'Then, three days since, the townspeople gathered for the wedding of the King's son, Prince Roland, to his ward, Princess Melisande. There was great rejoicing, for they were blithe and young, and loved by the people. But Princess Melisande was gone, stolen away in the night, none knew how. The King raved and tore his hair, and shut himself away through shame and grief, and that very morn Prince Roland set off for these wild forests of the West, to save his bride and slay the Thing.

'Two days he walked, and fought with the Giant Rodomont on his way; the Giant broke and fled, and so the Prince came to my very cottage, which you know is the last one of the village. A brave and honest face he had, and wore a white cloak without device and a shining helmet, with a sword of bite at his side. I told him what I could of the Tarn and the woods, and he told me the tale I tell you now.

'Then he set off by the path I spoke of, over the stream and across the meadows, past the stile to the rocks and the hills and the ancient oaks. And now 'tis the second night since his coming, and that is why I tell you that the Thing will soon be slain. Aye, very soon.'

The old woman's voice fell silent, and she nodded slowly backwards and forwards in her chair. The other women were staring at her, or into the fire, still lost in the tale, while the spinning wheels whirred comfortably on. The children, however, were exchanging looks of panic. David drew in his breath sharply, and the others turned to look at him, the spell now broken.

'But—' he began. 'The second night? And haven't you heard anything from him?'

Mother Margery was reaching for her pipe. 'Indeed, child, we have not. But do not fear. Prince Roland will be a fair match for the Worm, I warrant.'

'But what if he never gets near enough to fight it?' David protested. 'Look, read this!' And he rummaged through his rucksack for the terrible, prophetic pages that foretold Prince Roland's end.

The old woman shook her head as David held the pages out in the flickering glow of the fire. 'Nay, child, there is no light here for book-learning. What will be will be. Now, we'll have no more fears and fretting for tonight, for I see the Hounds have frighted you, and I have done you poor service with my tales of ghosts and Worms. Come, we'll lay more wood on the fire, and Winifred can toast us some griddle-cakes while I tell you tales of faraway lands.'

David still held the pages in his hand, but Charlotte tugged at his arm. 'It wouldn't do any good,' she whispered. 'It's up to us now.'

'You're right,' said David. He tried to rise, but his limbs were stiff and heavy, and he sank back down on his stool. The children's strength was spent, and tiredness held them fast in its coils.

'Nay, tomorrow will come soon enough,' said Mother Margery kindly. 'There's no good haste without strength for the journey.'

The children sat where they were, and wove in and out of sleep, each time dreaming that they had started up to rescue the Prince, and each time waking to find they had never moved. Then they found hot, buttered oatcakes in their hands. They ate them gazing into the fire, while Mother Margery's tales stole through their minds and came to life in the glowing shapes among the flames. They heard of genies and rocs, pygmies and gnomes, and the far-off tree where the phoenix rises unharmed from its fiery bed. Castles and dungeons, elves and enchanters, all played out their tales in the burning caverns and crags of the fire.

Then one of the logs became the Castle of Beltenebros, with a sea of flame all around. A valley led up beneath jutting cliffs to a great hollow log at the back of the hearth, with a gaping pit of fire at its heart. Deeper and deeper the children wandered into the scene. Far below the flames waited the Thing that Prince Roland would never see, while from the pit danced nine wisps of fire, the Sprites of the Tarn. The Prince had nearly come, and then sleep crept over them, and the vision passed away.

CHAPTER 7

The Nine Sisters

The next morning, David and Charlotte woke to find themselves lying on straw mattresses that had been drawn in front of the old woman's hearth. A pot was simmering over the fire, and cold autumn daylight was shining in at the window.

'Porridge for breakfast,' said Mother Margery, as the children rose to their feet.

'Thank you very much,' said David, 'and then I think we'd better be going.'

'And will you travel far today?' asked the old woman, ladling out the porridge and casting them a shrewd look.

'No,' said Charlotte. 'Not far, but we've something very important to do.'

Mother Margery nodded. 'You must do it, then. But if you need help and I can give it, seek me out. Past the stile, over the meadows, and by the bridge across the stream: you'll not forget. And you'll take some oatcakes with you, for hunger brings ill luck, they say.'

The children thanked her, and after a quick breakfast they took up their rucksacks and set off. They crossed the stream by a narrow footbridge, and then followed the path they had been told of the night before. They spoke little, but both were thinking of the Prince.

'She doesn't know about the Sprites,' said Charlotte after a while.

'And he's been here two nights now.'

'David, do you think they—do you think he—'

'Well, come on,' said David gloomily. 'We'll see.'

The woods loomed darkly up ahead. Soon they came to the stile, and then the path led into dense, towering holly thickets, mountains of greenery with a way cut through like a tunnel. The children pressed on, and in a while they came out into a scattered birch wood. The path climbed sharply, winding up between the rocks, flecked here and there with brilliant yellow birch leaves. Still there was nothing to be seen. No wind stirred, no bird sang, and there was no sign at all of the Prince or his camp.

The silence of the woods made them move stealthily. Crags rose ahead, and great boulders lay strewn over the hillside with grassy clearings nestling in between. Old oaks perched on the rocks, gripping them with roots as firm as iron. Then, just as they rounded a bend between two overhanging outcrops, they came upon the Tarn.

It lay as still as a mirror, with the crags and the forest rising up all round. The oaks stooped over it, straining at their reflections, while on the far side a great rocky hill fell sheer into the dark waters at its foot. From over the Tarn they heard the trickling of many streams, breaking eerily through the silence. There was not a soul in sight.

'Well?' said Charlotte, gazing miserably around.

'We'll explore—carefully. If we climb that big crag we might see some sign of the Prince.'

So they set off round the Tarn, picking their way through bracken and scrub and clambering over the rocks where they came down to the water's edge. They followed first a kind of ridge running all along one side of the Tarn, walling it off from the valley below. Then they dropped suddenly into a narrow gully, where three streams dashed down into the Tarn side by side. After they had crossed the last one, Charlotte stopped. The rushing and crying of the water rebounded from the rocks, and echoed all round them, louder and softer.

'Listen!'

'What?'

'Can't you hear voices? In the water?'

'Maybe . . . '

Charlotte broke into a run, and David followed her, up the gully's rocky walls and away from the shouting streams. They had come past the end of the Tarn now, and here the ground rose up to the big crag. At once they began to climb. From one ledge to another they scrambled up the rock-face, and then hauled themselves along a steep cut in the rock, clinging to the tough heather roots for support. In a few minutes they were up.

'That was a spooky place,' panted Charlotte, and David glanced back with a shiver at where the streams were still murmuring in their hollow. Then they looked round at the rocky hilltop.

'This rock is like a castle,' said David. 'See, those smaller crags that stick up at the corners are its turrets, and up here are the battlements. I think if I'd been the Prince I would have camped right here.'

'But he didn't want to be seen. He'll be in some clearing or hollow in the woods.'

'Well, let's have a look.'

So they scanned the entire view, from the flank of the hill that rose up towards the cliffs behind them, through the woods that were spread out between boulders and rocky hillocks on either side, down to the Wandering Valley lying at their feet.

'Not a thing,' said Charlotte. 'But a camp might easily be hidden behind one of the crags somewhere. If only it said in the book where it was!'

They carried on along the flat top of the crag, peering down into the forest as they went; but all they discovered were three more streams, gentle trickles that found their way down the mountainside and over the lip of the rock, dropping to the Tarn below in pattering waterfalls. At the last of them Charlotte paused, and followed it to the edge of the cliff.

'What is it?' asked David, hanging back. 'Come on, Charlotte: these streams aren't very nice.'

'I thought I heard laughter,' Charlotte replied. She was gazing after the waterfall, dripping down the mossy stone into the darkness.

'I can't see the stairs,' she murmured. 'The ones the ghosts are supposed to come up. But there's a dead log under water: over there, by the edge of the Tarn.'

'There can't be,' said David. 'The Tarn's supposed to be incredibly deep, and its sides are sheer.'

'Well, they can't be if I can see a dead log,' said Charlotte, drawing back slowly from the edge. 'And I can definitely hear laughter in the waterfalls.'

David grabbed her by the arm. 'Let's go, Charlotte. This isn't a good place to be.'

They made their way to the far end of the crag between the two turret-like projections and began to pick their way down the rock-face. When they were almost to the bottom, David came to a patch of bare earth on a narrow ledge. He stopped dead, looked at it twice, and then he called out in an unnatural voice.

'Charlotte! Come . . . come and look.' She came, and then they both stood and stared at the monstrous footprint. It was as long as an arm, and ended in three toes, each with a long, curving claw.

'What *is* it?' demanded Charlotte in horror.

'Something really, really horrible. Who knows? An ogre maybe?'

'But there aren't any in the book!' Charlotte burst out. 'Why aren't things the way they are in the story? And where are the stairs? And the Prince?'

'I don't know. Come on, let's get away from here.'

They scrambled the rest of the way down to the ground and made their way quickly round the last part of the Tarn. Soon they heard running water from ahead, and came to a group of springs. Two of them welled up from the grass beside a twisted alder, like wounds in the hillside; but the third rose with a low murmur from a dark pool overhung with ferns and dank, slippery rocks. They stopped and peered into the chasm, searching for the place where the water broke out of the rock, while the sound of the spring resounded around them, like a voice that urged and cajoled them to stay there always, forever gazing down into the black water, forever seeing nothing.

After a time, David snatched himself back from the hole, and tugged at Charlotte's arm. They looked around in panic, sure that they were being watched. Then suddenly they were running, jumping over stones and scrub as they rounded the last part of the shore. The cold sky, the water, and the woods were still, but all around rose the sound of the streams, bouncing from rock to rock and hurrying after them.

They ran until they had nearly reached the point where they first came to the Tarn. The streams were calling more faintly, and they slowed down. Then Charlotte glanced to one side and skidded to a halt.

'Look!'

'What?'

'The dead log!'

'I can't see anything.'

'No, it's gone. It was just by this rock, out in the Tarn.'

'It can't have been.'

'But it was.'

Then Charlotte nudged him in the back, and they started running again. 'It was the Thing! Don't you see?'

The Tarn was behind them now, but they fled on and on, as if all the dead had risen up from the waters and were gliding after them close behind. They left the path and plunged through mossy clearings and up broken hillsides, until at last they came to a part of the wood where enormous boulders stood like the houses of a deserted village.

'We should be . . . safe here,' panted David, as they came to rest in the angle between two great crags, overlooking a boulder-strewn slope. They got their breaths back, and then David said, 'Right. We can't find the Prince. We can't see the stairs, and there's some sort of three-toed monster about, as well as a Thing that looks like a log but isn't. And the whole place gives us the creeps. I think that about sums it up.'

Charlotte nodded, and then she looked down. 'David . . . we're too late, aren't we? The Prince isn't here. He's . . . dead.'

David frowned. 'Not necessarily. Two nights . . . the Sprites need time to trick him: they may not have done it yet. And this is a big wood, with plenty of places to hide. The fact that we haven't found him doesn't prove he isn't here.'

'Well, let's search, then!'

Again David frowned. 'I don't know. There are dangerous things about, and with all these rocks and hollows we might walk right past his camp and still not see it.'

'Then what *are* we going to do?'

'Don't worry. We'll find him, if he's— We'll find him. We know he's got to go to the Tarn, and he's got to go by moonlight. It's in the book: that's when he meets the Sprites. And if they haven't drowned him yet, they can't do it until tonight.'

'So we'll go there and watch for him?' Charlotte sat up excitedly.

'And warn him. That's right.'

'But it's hours till sunset! What are we going to do in the meantime?'

David rummaged in his pack, and handed Charlotte an oatcake. 'Eat . . . and rest. And make plans. Look, what if we *do* get to Prince Roland in time and save him from the Sprites? What happens then?'

Charlotte waved her oatcake. 'Well, then . . . he defeats the Thing and rescues the Princess.'

'Yes, but he's got to get under the Tarn somehow to do that. How's he going to do it? He didn't know the Thing lived under water until Mother Margery told him. He won't have brought any magic or anything.'

'And it's no good asking what happens in the book,' added Charlotte, 'because he doesn't get that far.'

David nodded. 'So it's up to us. We're the ones who can do magic.'

'Us?'

'Alchemy, I mean. That's our job for this afternoon: learn more about how this set works, and find some potion for breathing under water.'

So all that day they rested in their crevice, and chased the dancing script over the pages of their alchemy book. They read of many things, of concoction, maturation, and calcination, of the marriage of Sun and Moon, and the powers of Red Lion and Green, of Monk's Bane and Little King. Again and again they came upon mention of Death's Head, and the crucible that mirrors the world, and they thought more than once of Mother Margery's stories, and the Tarn, calm as a mirror, but with death at its bottom.

By evening they had read and reread most of the book. They had found recipes for storms and sickness, sunshine and healing, but not the thing they were looking for.

'Time to go,' said David, casting an eye at the setting sun. 'Let's take the set with us: you never know.' So David shouldered his rucksack, while Charlotte left hers tucked in the crack between the boulders.

They made their way cautiously back down through the wood, and settled themselves in a clump of bracken across the Tarn from the big crag. Then they waited. The shadows deepened, the first stars appeared in the darkening sky, and then a cold full moon rose slowly over the wood. A breeze sprang up which pierced them to the bone, and sent a sighing through the trees to mingle with the lonely babble of the nine streams; but the face of the Tarn never stirred.

'Nothing's going to happen,' said Charlotte. 'We've been waiting forever, and I'm freezing.'

'Just a bit longer,' said David.

Dusk was deepening into night, when a pale figure sprang silently out from the opposite shore. The children tensed, waiting for the splash, but the figure landed lightly on the water and skated out over its surface. Then two more leapt after it, out from the rocky gully where the first three streams flowed into the Tarn.

All three came spinning and wheeling over the water, now hidden in shadow, now a brilliant silver as they leapt clear into the moonlight, wild and free like rivers in spate. They skated round the reflected moon in an arc, scattering widely apart, and meeting only to scatter once more. Then the wind fell, and the sound of the three waterfalls carried louder from across the Tarn. There was a sound like a splash of playful laughter, and three more shapes sprang out from the shadows beneath the crag.

The newcomers tumbled and capered, sinking sometimes into the water and shooting up again like dolphins or seals, and then all six formed a line, sliding and whirling over the water, now near, now far; and just once they hissed past right under the children's hiding place, pale as clouds in the moonlight, with a sound like foam seething in the wake of a ship. The children watched entranced, and in their hearts both wanted to join the Sprites in their cold, wild dance, and play and leap over the still, unchanging water.

The dancers had almost completed their circuit of the Tarn when the children's eyes were drawn to the darkness below the far bank. There, just beside the springs, a pair of ghostly wisps floated up from the water like pale smoke. The dancers interrupted their flying, whirling course, and skated forward in line, while the wavering shapes drew aside. Between them something stirred, a thickening of the gloom, like a muffled figure waiting in the shadows and unwilling to be seen. Then a dark shape stepped on to the face of the Tarn, slow and solemn, glinting silver like the moon behind a cloud.

The others bowed low, and the last of the Nine Sprites advanced among them. The figure raised its arms, and all at once the whole troupe swung into a new dance, stately and measured, sweeping around the moon that shone in the midst of the Tarn in a great curve, like planets circling a sun, or a great clock that timed the motions of the heavens, faultless and precise.

The children lay mesmerized as the dance flowed on, round and round, like soundless music, stealing their senses away with its whirling, spinning movement. Soon it would have drawn them down to the water's edge, in their desire to be one with the dance, and perhaps they would have added to the number of those lost in the Tarn; but suddenly the pattern was broken. Something had happened to disturb the Sprites, and they scattered this way and that, flocking in groups, and darting uncertainly over the water. They kept glancing at the far side of the Tarn, and then David and Charlotte saw it too. There was a movement in the bushes down by the water. The Sprites pointed and hung back, all but their leader, who glided forward confidently towards the disturbance.

'What do you think it is?' whispered Charlotte.

'I'll bet you it's the Prince,' David breathed. 'Come on!' He crept back from the bracken, and Charlotte followed. Then there was a noiseless dash through the moonlight, scurrying along behind the ridge and past the head of the Tarn, then easing their way bit by bit up over the rocks above the far bank. They crept forward to the edge. Just below them a figure was standing between a pair of trees, silhouetted against the moonlit Tarn. A cloak hung over his shoulders and a helmet shone on his head: it had to be Prince Roland.

Beyond, the dark shape of the Sprite hovered over the water like a column of smoke, while her companions flitted to and fro behind, as if torn between boldness and fear. The Prince was gazing in silence as the Sprite drifted closer. She threw back her hood, and showed them a face as bright as the moon. Her lips curled into a smile, of mockery or mischief.

'Why have you come?' came the rippling, silvery voice. 'This is a lonely place, and treacherous by night. The rocks are slippery: many have been drowned.' Again she smiled, as if at some joke known only to herself.

'I know it,' said the Prince, and his voice sounded confident and loud. 'But I am bound to this place by my honour. The Foul Thing that dwells below these waters has stolen away my betrothed, the Princess Melisande, and I come here to rescue her, and to slay the beast.'

The Sprite drew back as if in alarm at his boldness, and then glided forward like smoke on a breeze. 'The Foul Thing!' she repeated, and was it admiration or contempt in her voice? 'You will slay it and save your betrothed?'

The Prince nodded grimly.

'But how will you bring it to battle?' the Sprite went on. 'I doubt not you will kill it if you do, for it is a cowardly thing, oh, very cowardly. But it dwells below, and how will you come there?'

There was a pause, as Prince Roland gazed at the Sprite, who met his look with wide eyes, kindly and anxious; but it struck the children with a chill of horror.

'You see you are lost, and have no knowledge what you will do.'

'A way will be found,' said the Prince.

The Sprite arched her brows. 'What way can you find, alone, without helpers?' She smiled again, and drifted closer still. 'But have no fear. I shall be your friend, to the end of your journey.'

The Prince started, and took a step towards the water. Charlotte clutched David's arm.

'It's happening! Let's warn him!'

'Not yet,' David whispered back. 'Let's watch.'

The Sprite had drawn back again. Her smile was bitter, and she nodded as she spoke. 'Oh, yes. We Sprites hate the Foul Thing as much as you.'

'Do you?' asked the Prince, with excitement and caution mixed in his voice. 'And could you . . . help me?'

For reply, the Sprite drew herself to the very edge of the bank, and now the children could see her features running and streaming over her face like water over stone. 'You must go down,' she said, 'down to the House at the Eye of the Storm. There the Thing dwells, and there his captive is kept. But the way is hard to find, and harder to travel. You must tread a perilous stair, round which a gale blows night and day. No living man has ever trodden it, and the way is known only to the dead.'

'But you know the way? You can show me?' demanded the Prince, and the Sprite laughed.

'I know the way. Yes, I shall guide you. I would do much for you, Prince Roland.' She smiled again, and the Prince put his hand to his sword as if he wanted to do battle then and there.

'When will you take me?'

'Soon, my Prince, soon. Yes, very soon.' She spread her arms and twirled round in a flash of silver and black, and the other Sprites glided closer, crying 'Eldest! Eldest! The dance!'

'Yes, my sisters,' sang the Eldest of the Sprites. 'It is time to dance, my Prince. Alas, you are made of clay, and cannot follow. Ah, if you could! What joys you would know then! To wheel on the black water below as the stars wheel in the blackness above! To be water dancing on water, and coldness in the cold of a winter's night: that is to be alive, well and truly! But yes, I will help you, man of clay. Return here another night. Come often; but never, never come in a storm.'

'Why not?' called the Prince, as the Sprites slipped away across the Tarn, spinning and flying, and the stately rhythm of the dance began.

'Be not too curious, my Prince!' the watery voice sang back, and then the nine sisters were gone, swallowed back into their dance by the night.

The children gazed after them, and again a longing came over them to be creatures of the elements, dancing over the dark water. When at last they lowered their eyes from the pale, dancing shapes, the Prince had gone. They slid quickly back off their rock.

'We've got to find him and warn him,' David whispered. 'Did you hear how taken in he was?'

'I was taken in myself,' said Charlotte, 'even though I *knew* they were evil.'

'I told you it wasn't so easy.'

'Well, come on. Let's search.'

Brilliant moonlight was falling on the wood, but the shadows among the boulders and knotted trees were pitch black. They called for the Prince in whispers, not daring to raise their voices for fear of the Sprites, and whatever worse might be about. Several minutes later they met again at the head of the Tarn, and looked at each other unhappily.

'Well, tomorrow we've *got* to find him,' said David. 'The next time he meets those Sprites is going to be his last.'

They made their way gloomily back up the boulder-strewn slope. When they came to the wedge between the two great rocks they stopped. Charlotte's rucksack had been dragged out from its corner, and lay with its contents spilled out on the ground. Their hearts were pounding as they looked all round for danger.

'Oh, look, look!' cried Charlotte, her eyes following a line of monstrous footprints, pressed deep in the moss between the rocks.

'Let's go,' said David. They were retreating down the slope, when a dark shape stepped between them and the moon. They heard the sound of a deep, rasping breath, and strong arms swung out towards them. They tried to dart aside, but the rocks shut them in, and the thing lunged forward with a bellowing laugh.

'Now I've got you!'

CHAPTER 8

Helga

'Put us down! Let us go!'

The thing, whatever it was, had swept the children up, one under each arm. They scratched and squirmed and pulled and kicked, but it was no use: they were held in a grip as firm as a vice. The moonlit forest brushed past their faces as the creature loped on, and every now and then they caught a sight of its broad, grinning mouth and snaggle teeth, its cauliflower nose and yellow, staring eyes.

'Hahahaha! Oh, hohohohoho!' bellowed the creature, shaking all over. 'It's no use trying that, my little friends! You're catched, fair and square! You're going where I'm going, yes indeed you are!' And it burst into another great guffaw of laughter.

'What are you going to do with us?' demanded David, thumping the thing's leathery hide with his fists.

'I'm taking you to Helga, of course,' the creature replied. 'She loves children. Now, stop your tickling, or it'll be the worse for you!'

'Why is it that everyone in this place eats children?' Charlotte moaned, and at this their captor broke out into a positive roar of mirth.

'Oh!' it rumbled at last, 'Helga will just *love* you two!'

After this, the children lapsed into an angry silence. To be caught and eaten was bad enough, but being laughed at as well was a bit too much. Back down the slope they were carried, and when they had nearly reached the Tarn, the creature turned aside. Soon they found themselves at the foot of the great crag that looked like a castle, where they had seen the first of the monstrous footprints.

'Nearly home, my dears!' called the thing, and lumbered right up to what looked like a solid rockface. Then the shadows swallowed them, and they slipped behind a fold of the rock into a tunnel. All was dark, and there was only the swaying motion and the huffing of the monster to remind the children of what was happening to them. Soon they began to climb, round and round. It was a long, spiral stairway, carved from the solid rock, and at every turn they passed a narrow window which let in a pale ray of moonlight.

Fear was beginning to take hold. 'Let us go!' yelled David again. 'You'll be sorry! You really will!' But the creature only chuckled. Now the stairs came to an end, and they suddenly came out into the open air. The children gasped. They were on a narrow bridge of rock that jutted out to one of the lone crags at the four corners of the outcrop. Above stretched the cold night sky, and below lay the Tarn, fathomless and dark. The monster walked out to the middle of the bridge and drew in a deep breath.

'Oh, Helga!'

At first there was no reply. Then they heard sounds of movement coming from the crag, and a rather cross voice called back, 'What is it, Horace?'

'I've got some children for you, Helga!'

'Children? Oh, Horace! For me?'

'Yes, Helga! Shall I bring them over?' And the beast strode on across the bridge, swaying once or twice, and giving the children a dizzying view of the abyss below. Soon they had passed under an arch and were inside the crag. They had a quick sight of rocky walls lit by a dim and flickering light, and then a second monstrous being was fussing round them, tickling their chins, and thrusting a leering face into theirs.

'Oh, Horace, they're the darlingest pets ever!'

The children kicked and shouted, and Horace blushed all over and murmured that he supposed they weren't that bad.

'Trollpuss!' cried Helga in reply, and gave Horace a smacking kiss on his shaggy cheek. 'They're just what I always wanted! I'll call this one Spot, and that one Patch!'

'Let us go!' shrieked Charlotte, as the truth dawned on her. 'We're not going to be pets of that nasty ugly old woman!'

'Ugly!' screamed Helga. 'Naughty rabbits! I'll serve you short rations of lettuce: that'll teach you to behave! Now, just put them in that box, Horace dear.' And with that she helped Horace to shove David and Charlotte into a large wooden hutch with air-holes drilled in the top and sides. The children fought every inch of the way, but it was no good. In a moment the lid went into place over their heads, and they were shut in, with only a dish, a jug of water, and a small pile of lettuce leaves for company.

'Now, Horace, this has all been so exciting I think I'll turn in for my beauty sleep. You know how bad excitement is for my complexion.' The creatures' voices grew fainter, the dim light receded, and then the children were left alone in the dark.

David heaved a deep sigh, and Charlotte muttered, 'This book's got far too many nasty surprises in it. Are they *trolls*? Where did they come from?'

'I think I remember,' said David slowly. 'The bit in

the story where Prince Roland first comes to the Tarn: doesn't it say, "keeping a careful look-out for trolls"?'

'You're right,' Charlotte agreed. 'Only in the story there weren't any after all. Why bother mentioning them if they weren't going to appear?'

'Well, they've appeared now.'

'Anyway, what are we going to do? Think of the Prince!'

'We're going to escape, of course.' David was pacing round the narrow space, his head bent down under the low ceiling. He shoved against the lid and the side panels, and stuck his fingers through the air holes, all in vain.

'What about the alchemy set?' asked Charlotte. 'Have you still got it?'

'Yes, if nothing's broken. But it's no use in the dark. We'll have to wait until morning.'

Charlotte sighed impatiently. 'Well, we might as well try and sleep, then.' So they settled down on the floor of the hutch and did their best. But all night they tossed and turned. First they lay awake thinking of potions and spells, and then they dozed, and the tangled, dancing script of the alchemy book whirled through their minds, all mixed up with the nine Sprites and the spinning wheels of the village women. Then they dreamt of their journey through the woods, and woke with a start to remember they were prisoners of the trolls.

It was a long night; but at last David surfaced to find the grey light of dawn filtering in through the holes in their prison. He sat up, and Charlotte stirred.

'What is it?'

'It's light—light enough to escape,' David whispered back. He moved along the walls of the hutch to see what he could spy through the holes. From outside there came a series of strange sounds: a low bubbling, and over it a clank and a clatter, and the murmuring of a voice. Charlotte crawled up beside him, and together they peered out at the troll's room.

Helga was seated with her back to them at a wide workbench. She was dressed in a patched greenish gown, and was mumbling over a great book in front of her, while her tail twitched over the floor with concentration. All around were potions and phials, jars and flasks; strings of dried things hung from the ceiling, and above everything else hung a great stuffed crocodile, its paws spread out in the air and its teeth bared in a fixed grin.

'She's a magician,' whispered Charlotte, and Helga started up from her reading.

'Are my lovey-ducks awake, then? Did they sleep well? Now, don't bother Mummy. She's very, very busy.'

'And what's Mummy doing?' called out David, with a wink to Charlotte.

Helga went on whispering words out of her book, and replied slowly, as if she were giving the children less than half of her attention, 'I'm making . . . myself beautiful.'

Charlotte repressed a snigger, and David called out again, 'Oh, really? And how are you doing that, Mummy?'

The she-troll's murmuring grew louder. ' . . . Eye of bat and tongue of toad, a mouse that's fond of sports . . . boil them up and you will have . . . a splendid cure for warts . . . What? Oh, by magic, my little chicks. Yes, I know I'm not very nice-looking, though it *was* naughty of Patch to say so. But never mind: Mummy's quite a

78

talented thing, you know. I've got ever so many spells and tricks, for shortening noses and rounding the points off ears . . . But it's a long, hard job, you know, chicks. I have to go all over for ingredients. Here's my winged shoes when I need to go up to the stars, and then sometimes I have to dive to the bottom of the sea after pearls and coral, and things like that.'

Helga turned back to her book, but the children's interest was aroused.

'What's that?' demanded Charlotte keenly. 'How do you do that?'

'I don't know if I should tell you,' retorted Helga severely. 'You were such a naughty pet to Mummy last night, Patch, using that nasty word like you did.'

'Oh, please, Mummy,' put in David, with another wink.

'Well, to please *you*, Spot. I just drink from this cup.' And she turned round on her stool and lifted down a curious, swirl-shaped cup. It shone with mother-of-pearl, and looked as if it had been made from some great sea-shell. Dolphins and mermen were carved on its side, and seemed to flow and chase each other round and round the rim.

'This cup belonged to Father Neptune himself,' boasted Helga, 'and he used to give it to his servants to drink from whenever he wanted to send them on some errand down into the depths of the sea. For you see, whoever drinks from this cup can breathe under the water just as if it was normal air.' She turned back to her book, placing the cup beside her elbow. 'Now leave me be, chickens. Like I told you, Mummy's very, very, extremely busy.'

'That's what we need,' whispered David. 'We've got to get hold of that cup.'

'And we've got to get out of this box, too,' added Charlotte. 'How are we going to do it?'

'It'll have to be alchemy,' David replied. 'You have a look through the book. I'm going to try something.' He cleared his throat, and then called out in an appealing voice, 'Mummy?' There was no answer. He tried again. 'Your magic sounds very interesting, Mummy. Would you like to see some of ours?'

But Mummy had lost interest in her pets. Without speaking, she got up and crossed over to the hutch, slid back the lid, stuffed some more lettuce leaves in on top of their heads, and then locked it back in place.

'That does it,' fumed David. 'Let's break out.'

'Look,' said Charlotte from the alchemy book. 'Here's an idea: fog.'

David's face broke into a smile. 'Not bad! But how do we get out of the hutch?'

'Something will turn up. That's phase two. And this is a recipe that doesn't need any heat. Listen. ''To brew a fog, wherewith to elude thine enemies. Pour two parts Vitriol into one of Orpiment, and concoct until they be both consumed; infuse thy Brimstone, and stand clear. Add thereto a sufficiency of water, for by water are fogs and mists bred.'' '

'Right,' said David. 'We'll use the bowl.' He chose the bottles from the alchemy set, and soon their potion was seething and smoking gently in the earthenware dish.

'Infuse thy Brimstone,' whispered Charlotte, sprinkling the yellowish powder out over the bowl, 'and stand clear!'

There was a whoosh of sparks, and a column of smoke began to curl up from the dish. David and Charlotte hung back against the wall of the hutch as the mixture fizzed and spat.

'What are you up to in there, lovey-ducks?' enquired Helga, in something of an absent tone.

'Nothing, Mummy,' sang out Charlotte, in much the same voice as she had often used at home. Meanwhile she had the jug in her hand, and began to pour a stream of water over the potion. There was a mighty hiss, and a dense cloud of mist rose up and blotted everything in the hutch from sight. Outside, the fog began to pour up out of the air holes, and Helga turned round with a scream.

'My little chicks! They're on fire!' She sprang from her stool, while the children emptied the last of the water over the fog potion.

'Horace! Horace! Come quickly!' Already the room was filling up with clinging, white vapour. Helga stumbled towards the door just as Horace burst in.

'What is it, angel-troll?'

'Fire!' screamed Helga, and there was the sound of pounding feet and the slamming of the door. The children held their breaths; the jug was empty, and already the fog was beginning to clear. Then they heard heavy footsteps: Horace was back. A moment later they were drenched to the skin, and fog was once more billowing out from the potion.

'Good old Horace!' shouted David. 'A whole bucket of water!'

'You're no use at all,' Helga was blubbering. 'My poor (sob) chickies! They'll burn all up!' She fumbled with the lid of the hutch, while Horace made excuses. A moment later the children were free. They scrambled up over the side, with the alchemy set safely stowed again in David's rucksack, and set off through the thick pea-soup that cloaked Helga's laboratory.

'Where are my chicks?' they heard her scream. 'They're gone! Burnt up!'

'No they haven't,' rumbled Horace. 'They've escaped, that's what, the little terrors!'

Meanwhile Charlotte was helping David up the rungs of Helga's stool. He pulled her up after him, and soon they were standing on the workbench beside the monstrous book. Through the fog loomed the face of a merman with sea-green beard and crown of seaweed. A dolphin reared up behind, and David grabbed the cup of Neptune. It was twice the size of a normal cup, and he struggled with it back down on to the stool, which wobbled as he landed on it.

'Over there!' shouted Horace, and blundered off in their direction.

'Ouch! You trod on my tail!'

'I didn't mean to, dearest.'

'That's beside the point,' Helga complained, and they heard the sound of the she-troll sucking her bruised appendage.

'They're getting away!' bellowed Horace, who was ranging all round the room, tripping over the stool, knocking over this and smashing that. The fog drifted and rolled in clouds, showing a brief glimpse of the smiling crocodile overhead, or the flailing arms of the angry troll. The children darted from one part of the floor to another, afraid more than anything of being trodden on.

'Stop it, Horace! Oh, you oaf, what have you broken now? Open the door, and let the fog out!'

'No, Helga, don't!' yelled the troll, but Helga had reached the door and was fumbling for the knob.

'The little imps! Nasty sorcerous little creatures! Call *me* ugly!' The door was open, and the next moment the children were through it and out into the cold morning air over the bridge of stone.

'Horace! There they go!'

'I told you they'd escape.'

'No, you didn't. Anyway, after them!'

David and Charlotte hurried across the bridge, which shook to the tread of the trolls, shambling along close behind.

'Which archway?' gasped David. There were three, all opening into the wall of rock ahead, and no way of knowing which led to the spiral stair.

'Try the right,' Charlotte cried, and they ran on into the darkness. The passage ran straight, and then all at once they stumbled over some steps that led down, turning as they went.

'Thank goodness!' breathed David, as they hopped round and round the central column of the stairs, down and down. The trolls could be heard breathing heavily up above, and picking their way more slowly.

'David,' Charlotte whispered after a while. 'Something's wrong: there are no windows!'

'You're right. This isn't the right staircase!'

They plunged on through the darkness, flying round the central pillar in a dizzying whirl, while the sounds of pursuit grew fainter from up above. At last there was a glimmer of light, and suddenly they were out on a ledge, with the still waters of the Tarn below, and the far shore gleaming golden in the morning light. They gasped, and pressed themselves against the rock to save themselves from falling.

'Which way now?' Charlotte demanded. The ledge led off to left and right, snaking along the rockface in a line that could hardly be seen.

'This way!' shouted David, and set off in the direction that led away from Helga's tower.

'They'll never follow us along here, anyway,' said

Charlotte. But in this she was wrong. The trolls came out from the passage and immediately set off after them, edging their way along and clinging to handholds further up the cliff for support. They were at home on the rock, and soon had very nearly caught up.

'Down there!' called Charlotte, after a frantic glance back at their pursuers. Beneath them ran another ledge, right where the rock made its final plunge down into the dark waters below. A bulge in the cliff hid the trolls from sight, and at once the children set about climbing down to the lower ledge, easing themselves from one foothold to the next. The ledge was wider than it had looked, and in a moment they lay on it gasping for breath, while the trolls paused overhead, baffled.

'Look!' whispered David. Leading down to the water there were some steps: three of them, and then a fourth just below the surface, and the ghost of a fifth almost swallowed up in darkness.

'It's the stairs!' Charlotte whispered excitedly. 'David, we've found them!'

'Shh!'

Above them, the trolls were having a conference.

'They've gone down to where the ghosts come up,' said Helga.

'I'm not following them down there,' said Horace emphatically.

'Oh yes you are.'

'No, I'm not.'

'You are.'

'Oh, all right then.'

Then they heard Horace grumbling and muttering, and sliding cautiously down the rockface above their heads. David and Charlotte looked from side to side for a new way of escape.

'There's got to be some way out,' whispered Charlotte. 'The ghosts must have some route from here to the village.'

They crept along the ledge, and soon came to an opening in the rock. Mossy slime hung about it where one of the three waterfalls trickled down into the water. A damp and musty smell came from inside, and a faint glow lit up the walls. The children hesitated.

'Well,' said David, 'it's the trolls or the ghosts.' Footsteps were coming along the ledge; quickly they slipped into the darkness. The sound of their breathing echoed in the tunnel, while from behind they heard the pattering of the waterfall, mixed with the voices of the trolls.

'I'm not going in there. I am *absolutely* not going in there.'

'You must, Horace. There isn't any danger.'

'But the ghosts, Helga! The horrible, frightful ghosts!'

'They're all back under water by now, you silly pet. They never stay out after dawn.'

'There's one that does. You know who I mean: the wild one, the one who came of her own free will. I've seen her out in the dawn, lingering in the caves. I tell you I can't do it, Helga!'

Then they heard Helga murmuring low. Soon Horace began to chuckle and whine, and the children knew she was talking him round.

'We've got to hurry,' whispered David. Their eyes were getting used to the dark, and now they saw that there were greenish luminous streaks along the walls of the tunnel, and feebly gleaming footmarks on the rocky floor.

'David . . . do you think those were made by the ghosts?'

'Just . . . run,' David replied. They hurried on faster, and now they could hear the trolls coming after them behind.

'Haw! You call me such pretty names, Helga!'

'Yes, Horace. Now be quiet and lead the way. My pets are escaping.'

The trolls huffed after them, and the children ran on, following the turns in the passage by the glowing streaks on the walls. They turned a corner, and ahead saw a glare of light.

'We're nearly out!' cried David, but a moment later he saw he was wrong.

'It's coming towards us!' yelled Charlotte.

'Face the rock and close your eyes!' David shouted, and they pressed themselves against the side of the passage as the bright shape rushed down on them with a deathly scream. Its mouth was wide and its eyes stared, and pale fingers trailed the tunnel walls, leaving the luminous marks they had seen. In a moment it was upon them. They put their hands over their heads, and with a shriek and a chilling rush of air the ghost was gone.

Then there was another scream, a double trollish scream of pure terror. Heavy feet stampeded into the distance, mingled with hoots and yells of fear, and the high-pitched wailing of the ghost. The sounds died away, and there was silence. The children slowly lowered their hands and eased themselves away from the rock. Then they made their way tremblingly along the rest of the passage, and fell panting on the dewy ground, drinking in the clear morning air.

CHAPTER 9

To Brew a Storm

'Now for the Prince!' cried Charlotte, as they hurried away from the menacing crag. 'And I don't care if we've got to search every inch of this wood!'

'There *could* be more trolls about,' David began doubtfully.

'They won't get over their shock for ages. Come on: we've got the Cup of Neptune, and we even know where the stairs are. All that's left is to find the Prince.'

'All right. Let's get your rucksack first.'

So they went back up the hill to the spot where Horace had captured them the night before. Charlotte stowed everything back in her pack while David gazed out over the trees.

'Look! What's that?'

'It's smoke: a campfire!'

'Come on!'

They bounded down the hillside, and plunged off through the forest. Soon they were deep in the maze of boulders and glades, and the column of smoke was hidden from sight. They spent some time casting about this way and that, and David had just set off in a new direction when he heard a voice from behind.

'A child! Or are you an elf? Speak!'

He ran back through the trees, and in a moment joined Charlotte on the edge of a clearing. Before them was a young man with a smiling face, sitting cross-legged on the ground and frying some cakes for his breakfast. He wore a white cloak and a shirt of mail; a sword was at his side, and a helmet, blanket, and pack lay nearby.

'Well? Have you the power of speech?'

'You must be Prince Roland,' Charlotte said at last.

'A prophetess!' replied the Prince, with a twinkle in his eye. 'And will you share my breakfast with me, my young wood-elves?'

The children came and sat by the fire. 'Thanks very much,' said David. 'We've had nothing since last night but some lettuce leaves. It's a long story.'

The Prince eyed him with curiosity, and handed each of them a hot griddle-cake. The children watched him all the time, not knowing how to begin. After a while he spoke again.

'The woods are beautiful, are they not? But they are dangerous, too. Much too dangerous for babes to be wandering in. Do you not know there are trolls living in the rocks?'

'Oh, we know all about *them*,' said Charlotte scornfully.

'Yes,' added David, coming round to the subject. 'The trolls aren't the problem.'

Prince Roland's eyes opened wider. 'And will you tell me what is?'

'The Tarn,' said David. 'In particular, the Sprites.'

'Ah!' sighed the Prince. 'The Sprites! They are the most beautiful creatures in nature! Their movements, flowing like water, their grace, their smiles . . . ' He gazed into the distance, and the children exchanged frightened looks.

'More beautiful than Princess Melisande?' asked Charlotte pointedly.

'Ah, now you would have me compare the human with

the divine! But have no fear: I have not forgotten my quest. The Sprites will aid me. Eldest has promised.'

'I know,' said David. 'We were there.'

'Don't trust her,' said Charlotte.

'She means to drown you!'

'By tomorrow, you'll be dead!'

The Prince looked in amazement from one face to the other. 'Nay, children, children! What tale is this?' And something in his tone made them think of King Stephen, closing his ears to their warnings in the dark hall of Beltenebros.

'It's no tale,' said Charlotte. 'What makes you think the Sprites would help you? Don't you know about the ghosts? All those people—drowned!'

'Aye, I have heard tell of the ghosts,' replied the Prince. 'The Tarn is a fickle place: Eldest said as much. The rocks are slippery, and folk will be foolish. Are not the Sprites more like to be the Worm's foes than its friends? Whence come your suspicions? What evil can there be in such beauty?'

'That's just how they manage it,' said David. 'They could never do so much harm without trickery.'

'I trust to my sword,' said the Prince, giving it a slap. 'And 'tis the only way: except by magic, none may pass below the Tarn. Eldest swore she would guide me down the stair.'

'Yes—dead!' cried Charlotte.

'Even if it *was* the only way, that wouldn't make it the right one,' said David. 'And anyway, it's not. Look!' And he held up the Cup of Neptune. 'Anyone who drinks from this can breathe under water, and we know where the stairs are, too! Please, you've got to believe us: we'll take you there!'

The Prince frowned. 'Whence had you this cup?'

'We got it from the trolls,' answered Charlotte. 'They use it for their magic. Won't you believe us?'

'I believe you mean to act honourably,' said the Prince slowly. 'But before I trust a devilish sorceror of a troll, I would trust the Nine Sisters of the Tarn. Are not the trolls a hundred times more likely to be treacherous than they?'

'Wait till you've read this,' said David, reaching into his rucksack. But the Prince had heard enough.

'Nay, I will hear no more of it. Be off with you back to the village, and trifle no more in these matters. I shall fare well enough, I promise you.'

He gave them a stern look, and the children gazed at him pleadingly for a long moment. Then David tugged at his sister's arm, and they turned back into the forest.

'Why won't he believe us?' Charlotte burst out. 'Why won't anyone?'

David was silent. Then, when they were nearly back to the Tarn he said, 'Look, what are we going to do? We can't just wander around. The trolls may be about.'

'Well, we'll camp somewhere, then. What about the holly thickets, down towards the village?'

'Right. Then we'll make plans.'

So they trudged downhill to the forbidding wall of hollies that lay between the birch wood and the fields. They burrowed in under the branches, and settled themselves in a kind of cave deep inside the thicket.

'We'll be safe enough here at least,' said David.

Charlotte was staring moodily, her chin on her fist. 'It'll be tonight,' she said. 'I know it will.'

'Well, what are we going to do? Think!'

'Alchemy.'

'Yes, but what?'

'I don't know.'

David got out the book, and they ran all through it searching for a plan.

'A sleeping charm . . . we could put him to sleep?'

'We'd be in just the same fix when he woke up again.' They read on in silence.

'A storm,' murmured David. 'What did the Sprite say about a storm?'

'She said he wasn't to come in one,' said Charlotte. ' "Never, never come in a storm." '

'And why not?' David pursued.

'I don't know. Maybe they do something nasty then.'

'Maybe so,' David went on, with rising excitement. 'And if they did, and if Prince Roland saw them, he might find out what they were really like!'

'That's two ifs,' said Charlotte, 'and the third one is *if* there's a storm.'

'But there will be,' cried David. 'We'll make one!'

Charlotte's eyes opened wide. 'Quick, where does it say how to do it?'

David leafed quickly through the pages. ' "To brew a storm," ' he read. ' "Will ye make the winds to rage, and set the elements at war? Then let your crucible be fired well, and infuse therein the Powder of the Cave and Seed of Saturn . . . Let them be married well, and a grain of Potash added thereto will unloose the winds from their subterranean vaults." '

'Excellent!' said Charlotte, reading over his shoulder. 'And look: "Will ye have lightnings, and fiery corposants that dance like devils about the masts of ships? Add then the ash of Jove's oak, burnt by his own fire." What does that mean?'

'I don't know,' said David thoughtfully. 'Never mind, we'll get everything else ready first. We're going to need a cauldron.'

'Mother Margery,' said Charlotte. 'She said we could go to her for help.'

'Let's go, then!'

They scrambled out from the holly thicket and ran down the path, over the stile and out of the woods. Soon they had crossed the stream and were knocking on Mother Margery's door. They heard a coughing and a shuffling from inside, and then the door was opened.

'Back again, are you? Have you done what you set out to?'

'Not quite yet,' said David, 'but we'd like to borrow a pot from you, if we could—rather a big one.'

'A pot, would you? Well, I've got an old one I can spare. And would you like anything to go in it? Potatoes, turnips?'

'No thank you,' said Charlotte. 'We're providing all that sort of thing ourselves. But if you *did* have any more of those nice oatcakes . . .'

'A stranger pair of children I've never seen,' said Mother Margery with a shake of her head, as David and Charlotte staggered back off to the woods with the great black cauldron between them.

At last they set it down on the rock above Prince Roland's hiding place by the Tarn, and leant panting against its side.

'Now let's get a move on,' said David. 'There are lots of things we need. We can have lunch while we're looking—and watch out for trolls.'

They combed the woods for their ingredients. First there were round pebbles to find, and after that they had to climb right up to the foot of the cliffs to cut a rowan stick to stir their brew with. All the time David was repeating the words of the alchemy book to himself, and when they passed a tall stump with a burnt top he suddenly knew what they meant.

'That's it! Jove's oak, burnt by his own fire! It means struck by lightning: Jove is Jupiter—god of thunder.'

Charlotte stared up at the tree. 'So we've got to climb it. Is that what you're saying?'

They tried in vain to get a foothold, but in the end Charlotte managed to scrape away a handful of the charcoal and ash by standing on David's shoulders. By now the sun had set behind the cliffs, and they hurried to light a fire under the cauldron and fill it from the Tarn, a cup at a time.

Their brew was just beginning to bubble when they heard a movement below the rock, and Prince Roland stole into position.

'Shall we begin?' whispered Charlotte.

'Not yet,' David replied. 'If we start too soon, the Sprites may not come out.'

They strained their eyes, scanning the darkening shores of the Tarn. The moon rose, and at last a pale shape darted out from the shadows over the surface of the water. Just as before, the wild Sprites of the Streams led the dance; then the playful Sprites of the Falls joined in, and lastly the sombre Sprites of the Springs, led by the cloaked figure of Eldest.

'Now,' said David, stuffing more wood under the cauldron, so that the fire began to blaze up around its sides. Charlotte meanwhile picked out two of the bottles from the alchemy set and pulled off their stoppers.

'Powder of the Cave . . . Seed of Saturn,' she whispered, and from one bottle a greyish dust sparkled down into the potion, mingling with a golden rain from the other.

' "Let them be married well," ' said David. He stirred

the brew with the stick of rowan, but the grey and the gold swirled round in two separate bands of colour. David frowned.

'David!' hissed Charlotte from the edge of the rock. 'It's Eldest!'

He crept up beside her, and there below hovered the Sprite, a mysterious smile on her face, and all her tall figure draped in black.

'You have returned, my Prince!'

'Yes,' said the Prince, with perhaps a touch of suspicion in his voice. 'And I would ask you to guide me to the place where dwells the Worm, as you promised me.'

'I promised you that!' the Sprite repeated. 'I shall promise you more, my Prince!' She flowed up to him like a wave, and broke before his face into a thousand hissing drops of foam, which pattered back into the Tarn with the sound of many laughing voices. Then the dark form of Eldest curled up again from the water like a fountain. Her face shone, and her silvery hair played all round it like the spray that drifts up from a waterfall.

'I am water,' she said, 'and so shall you be. You will put aside your garment of clay, and become one of us. Come, my Prince!'

And she stretched out her arms, which ebbed and flowed in the air like streams. The Prince hung back, but went on staring, fascinated.

'Do you doubt me, my Prince? Nay, come. This Tarn cradles the bones of many mortal fools. But to you I offer life. Come, join our dance, and later I shall take you to the House you seek. None may travel there but the Sprites of the water, and the dead.'

'And might I . . . really be like you?' whispered the

Prince, while the Sprite swayed and flowed over the water, smiling and beckoning all the time.

'And join the dance,' crooned the Sprite. 'Yes, my Prince. Come, it takes but a kiss.'

The Prince stared at her stupidly, and took a step closer to the water's edge.

'David!' Charlotte whispered urgently. 'It's happening! The potion!' They darted back to the cauldron, and set to stirring it, but still the grey and the gold refused to mix.

'A kiss, my Prince!' the Sprite's words floated up from below, and Charlotte glanced over the rock to where the Prince was edging closer and closer to the Sprite's outstretched arms.

'Hurry!' Charlotte hissed, and David put more kindling under the pot, and stirred the potion furiously until the colours swirled and eddied round and round, close but always apart. They heard the Prince's slithering footsteps from below, and Charlotte ran back to the edge. The Sprite stretched out her arms and came gliding up close, her pale lips parted, and the Prince reached forward for his kiss.

'It's cleared!' cried David, and threw in a handful of Potash. Just as Prince and Sprite were about to meet, a cold gust of wind blew through the wood, and they drew apart. The Prince turned his face towards the freshening breeze, and Eldest looked around in dismay. Then David stirred the pot with the rowan stick. The wind picked up from a sigh to a growl, setting the tops of the oaks bending before it. The other Sprites flew forward across the water, and Eldest turned a frightened face to the Prince.

'Go!' she commanded.

Prince Roland stood rooted to the edge of the Tarn. 'Why?'

'Go! The storm is coming . . . go, now!'

But still the Prince stood, while the Sprites flitted to and fro in agitation.

'Eldest! Eldest!'

'Now!' Charlotte shouted. She threw in Brimstone and Hellebore, and David gave the cauldron a mighty stir. Clouds boiled up from the horizon, streaming across the moon and blotting it from sight. The winds fell on the wood in earnest, screaming down from every side. The trees roared and howled like an angry crowd, and dead leaves rattled over the ground, driven into frenzied flurries as the gusts and eddies strove and stormed one against another.

Now the Sprites glided off across the Tarn, and tore the night with an unearthly scream. They raged and leapt and flew with the wind, at one with the storm, and forgetful of the Prince who still stood open-mouthed by the shore.

'We need light,' shouted Charlotte over the noise of the wind. She tipped the ashes from the blasted oak into the potion. At once there was a tremendous clap of thunder, the ground shook, and the children fell flat. Then there was another and another. Forks and sheets of lightning played across the sky, and balls of fire were hurled to and fro by the winds. Below, the Sprites gathered behind Eldest and swung into a dance, not calm and measured as before, but fierce and free. The wind was shrieking in the trees, and over its din they heard the singing of the Sprites.

'And when I have kissed him, sisters, sisters, what shall I do?'

'Drown him, Eldest, drown him, drown him,' sang the other Sprites in chorus.

'And what of his bones, sisters, sisters? Where will they go?'

'Down, Eldest, down they will go, to the House at the Eye of the Storm, and the Worm will feast on his flesh.'

The children turned away with a shiver. Then David threw the pebbles in, and the hail came pelting down over the wood, whitening the ground in the fleeting moonlight and hissing in the fire. The Sprites let out another shriek, and went raging all round the Tarn, shooting up into the air and pounding down with the hail, then leaping up again as fountains and flying on like streams in spate, or battering the shore like ocean breakers.

The lightning flashed, and now the Sprites took on every kind of monstrous form. They were a fire, a hangman, an army sacking a city. After that a heavy gloom spread over the Tarn, and the rain came down. Then the children heard the undergrowth snapping below them. They looked down, and saw Prince Roland break from his hiding place and run blindly off through the trees.

David and Charlotte crept away from the Tarn, while the Sprites howled and danced all night and the rain fell, and their cauldron sat on the hillside, now black and cold.

CHAPTER 10

The Winding Stair

Next morning the wind was still roaring in the trees, and squalls of rain came spattering down from a grey sky. David and Charlotte had spent an uncomfortable night huddled in their sleeping bags in the holly thicket with their anoraks wrapped round them, and were not sorry when it was dawn.

'Here,' said David. 'That's the last of the oatcakes. Then we'll find the Prince.'

'And give him the cup. Then we go home: is that the plan?'

David looked at her.

'It's just . . . I've been thinking. One person alone isn't enough: you can get taken in. It's not as if it was just a fair fight. And . . . don't you think we should go with him?'

David was pondering. 'Down into that dark, watery hole—full of bones and ghosts. It'll be dangerous. Much more dangerous than anything so far.'

'That's why he needs our help. They say the dragon's horribly cunning, and there are still the Sprites. There's no point in having come if he gets killed now.'

David frowned, and then began to nod. 'It'll be harder than it has been, though. The story won't be any help, and we can't take the alchemy set under water.' He slid the lid off the set and gazed at its contents.

'Look,' said Charlotte, and took out the pair of bottles labelled 'Alkahest' and 'Shape-Changer'. 'These'll be all right: they're sealed in glass. And we can take this, too.'

She drew out the large and curious egg, and handed all three to David. He examined them for a moment, and then slipped them in his rucksack.

'All right: let's go.' They buried the alchemy set in the leaf litter along with Charlotte's rucksack and crawled out from the thicket.

They found Prince Roland camped in the same place as the day before. This time there was no fire; he wore a harrowed expression, and his drawn sword was stuck in the ground by his side. He turned to gaze on them as they approached.

'*Now* will you believe us?' demanded Charlotte, and the Prince nodded grimly.

'Then follow us,' said David.

Prince Roland rose to his feet, drew his sword from the ground, and followed the children from the clearing.

'Aren't you going to put your sword away?' asked Charlotte, as they neared the shore of the Tarn.

The Prince shook his head. 'I have sworn an oath. I shall not sheathe my sword of bite until the deed is done. No more will I be led astray from my quest.'

By now they were skirting the crag where the trolls lived, and the children began to scan the face of the rock for the entrance to the ghosts' tunnel.

'There!' cried Charlotte, pointing to a group of faint green lines that led round a bulge in the stone.

'I see nothing,' said the Prince. 'Mean you to lead us into the house of the trolls?'

'We'll see some worse places than that,' said David, as they passed behind the fold in the rock and into the dank passage beyond. The ghosts had been out again in the night; the storm had brought them trudging up the stair, and all night they had gone howling through the wood and flocking round the houses of the village in their longing and despair. By dawn the weary troupe had gathered again at the entrance to their cave, and glided back through the tunnel to their home below the water. The marks along the walls and floor glowed freshly, and a coldness hung in the air that froze their spirits.

After a time, the sound of running water came from ahead, a breeze blew in their faces, and there was a grey glow of daylight in the distance. Soon they came out on to the ledge. A chill wind whipped past them, and all around was the angry roaring of the streams, swollen by the night's rains. Prince Roland gazed down into the dark water, and shivered.

''Tis cold as death,' he murmured. 'I have come close enough to drowning in its waters. How are we to pass below?'

For answer, David drew the Cup of Neptune from his rucksack. He dipped it in the icy water of the Tarn and handed it to the Prince.

Prince Roland looked at the cup uncertainly for a moment, while mermen and tritons wallowed round its sides in uncanny motion. Then he took it, closed his eyes, and drank.

'A warming draught,' he said with surprise.

'Now it's our turn,' said David, taking the cup from his hands.

'Nay,' protested the Prince. 'You are but children: wise ones, I grant, but children just the same. You have set me on my road, and I thank you. But you must not follow.'

'We're not leaving you now,' said Charlotte. 'You need us.'

'It's not just a matter of fighting,' added David.

100

The Prince seemed to ponder a moment, and then he smiled at them. 'Let it be so. Drink!'

David took the cup, filled it, and drank. Then he passed it to Charlotte. The charmed water seemed to flow all through their bodies, making them feel drowsy and warm. Then all three turned to look at the mossy steps that ran down to the water and disappeared in darkness. As they watched, the clouds rolled away from the sun, and the water shone clear. The winding stair curled round and round the side of the Tarn, deeper and deeper, until it blurred into the faint, blue depths, many fathoms below. Then the clouds spread back over the sun, and darkness once more engulfed the Tarn.

'I shall lead,' said the Prince, and stepped forward to where the stairs began. His sword brushed the wall of the cliff, and at the third step the water washed over his feet. He hesitated, then went on. The water rose up his body, and in a moment he was gone.

Charlotte went next. When the water welled over her ankle she let out a gasp. 'Oh! It isn't wet!'

'What do you mean?'

But Charlotte had gone on another two steps, and then two more, feeling the water rise around her like mist. At last it closed over her head. She held her breath, fully expecting to choke; then she took a gulp, and cried out. David heard her voice echoing up from below.

'David! I can breathe! It's . . . like fog!' He followed, and soon vanished under the Tarn in his turn. The water clung to them, damp and heavy like a chill November morning, and not at all like real water. The grey sky and the crag glimmered above, while below stretched the void, a black pit without a bottom.

Prince Roland was striding ahead, and the children hurried after him, picking their way down the slimy steps. The ghosts' fingermarks glittered on the rocky walls, rippling and changing in the fitful light. At one moment they were green, then blue, and then the whole wall of rock was lit with a reddish glare, as if they were passing by some giant's forge, and their shadows leapt high above them, stretching longingly towards the air.

'This is a strange place,' Charlotte whispered, and David followed her eyes off into the murk, where hazy shapes were forming and changing, drifting apart and gathering together, slowly becoming more distinct. The sound of the streams still echoed down from above, and over it they thought they could hear the distant sound of voices, speaking in whispers that rose up from the bottom in broken snatches.

Then a shadow passed over them, and all three turned their heads up towards the sky. A dark shape was circling overhead, like a spiral of rope, or a dark dye stirred into a liquid. It slipped aside into the shadows, but the three of them stood still, peering after it.

'There!' David pointed off to the side. The water gleamed and rippled like old bottle glass, green and flawed; bubbles swirled past, and a shape swam up out of the gloom. Before them, just out of reach, hung the great head of the Thing. Its yellow eyes shone like lamps, inquisitive, cunning, and empty of feeling. Long whiskers trailed from its jaws, and the snakelike body sparkled with many colours. It remained motionless, only flexing its front legs slightly as it fixed the Prince with its soulless stare.

'Fight!' shouted the Prince, breaking the silence at last. 'Come! Fight me, Worm!' But the Thing made no movement and no reply. The water swirled in front of its yellow eyes, and then it gave a great thrash of its glittering coils and flowed off into the gloom. Its shadow played over them for a moment like a flame, and was gone.

'Why will you not fight?' shouted Prince Roland, gripping his sword and peering away into the darkness.

'It won't fight,' said David. 'Not yet. It's got a few more tricks in store first, I should think.'

Prince Roland looked at David and nodded. 'Wisely said, child. Yet a time will come when I shall meet it with honest blows.' He set off once more down the winding stair, and the children followed.

The strangeness of the place increased as they went. Before long they felt a clammy kind of wind against their backs, and they realized that the water of the Tarn was beginning to turn. At first it was so gentle as hardly to be felt, but soon there was no mistaking it: they were coming to the great whirlpool that blew round and round the bottom, the storm that never rests, of which Mother Margery had told them.

All the time the shapes and the voices were growing clearer. Once they heard sounds of laughter and the clinking of glasses, and the water tasted of wine, while the blurred shapes of merry-makers drifted across the emptiness by their side; then the vision faded, and in its place came the distant clanging of bells and sailors' cries, a taste of salt and a glimpse of foundering ships, far off over a storm-racked sea.

After that the water cleared, and they saw the other side of the shaft glimmering as if through a crystal, with tier on tier of steps slanting across its face. There was a screaming from above, and nine shapes swooped past them, spiralling down and down out of sight.

'Trouble in store,' said David. 'We'll see more of the Sprites before we've done.'

The others made no reply. Soon all their attention was needed to avoid being swept off the stairs by the gale that was raging harder every minute. It pressed against their backs, forcing them into a run, and it teased at their feet as they slipped from one step to the next. On and on they sped, with the wind in their ears, and a shifting wall of colours and visions at their side.

Suddenly the gloom parted, and the wind dropped. The churning well of blackness below them was gone: instead they found themselves in a huge, echoing stairwell, still tripping downwards from step to step, with an iron handrail on one side, and a towering whitewashed wall to the other. David reached his hand out to the rail, but then drew it back.

'It can't really be there,' he said. 'None of this is real: it's all illusions.'

'It's like a crucible,' said Charlotte. 'Do you remember what the alchemy book said?'

'"Our crucible is the world,"' David quoted, '"and in it all things are mirrored." Yes, I remember.'

'This Tarn is just like that. "Tinctured with many colours, which come into being and pass away."'

Prince Roland cast a strange look back at the children. 'You are learned in arcane matters, for ones so young.'

'Oh, we're not *real* experts,' Charlotte replied, and just then the mysterious stairway entered an archway, so that now there were walls on both sides. A little further on they came to a doorway on the left, leading into what should have been the empty void of the Tarn.

'I wonder,' said Charlotte. 'Where do you think it leads?'

'Nowhere,' said David. 'It isn't real. Come on!'

'But it feels real,' Charlotte insisted, stroking the wooden doorknob with her hand. 'I wonder what it would be like to be inside something that feels real, but that you know isn't?'

'Stop, Charlotte! Don't do it!'

But Charlotte had already turned the knob, and stepped through the door into the bare, shadowy corridor beyond.

'Come back!' shouted David, and reached his hand out after her. But his fingers passed through the knob without touching it, and the vision swayed and dissolved as the storm began once more to blow. Bubbles eddied past, and the ghostly lines on the wall trailed gleaming into the distance. The current swept David on, with only a last despairing look back at the spot where his sister had disappeared.

Meanwhile, Charlotte had forgotten to think about her companions. The dim, silent corridor entranced her, and a faint light from up ahead lured her on. Soon she came out into a vast, dome-shaped hall, lit with a greyish glare from distant skylights above. Her steps echoed strangely as she wandered out into the hall, gazing up at the maze of balconies and stairs that wound up around the walls, and marvelling more and more.

When she reached the centre of the floor she stopped. She could hear nothing now but the beating of her heart. The stillness and bleakness of the place held her in a kind of spell, after the roaring of the water and the hurried, slippery descent down the winding stair.

Then she began to hear voices. They were too low for her to catch any words, but came whispering and mumbling from all around, and with them the sound of footsteps. Charlotte hurried across the floor and hid behind a column, but still there was nothing to be seen. The steps echoed and boomed round the empty hall, rose up to the dome and were thrown back again, multiplied and distorted, until it sounded as if great crowds were on the move, up and down and round, while a host of voices whispered to each other urgently to make haste.

Then the sounds died away; a cold wind blew through the hall, and Charlotte heard something new. It was the ring of a slow, heavy tread mounting a stair, and then a door was opened somewhere above, and there was silence. Charlotte held her breath, and somehow she knew that it was the Thing that had come. A voice rang out in the stillness, clear and cold.

'Who is it that comes, my daughters?'

A woman's voice answered, 'Strangers, father.'

'And why do they live? You did not drown them, Eldest daughter.'

'They are wizards, father. They made a storm.'

'So? And my daughters were cheated!' There was a pause, after which the Thing began again, 'They come to kill me, my daughters.'

'They shall not do that,' replied the Sprite quickly.

'And what will you do to work their ruin?'

'There are a thousand ways, father,' Eldest replied, 'a thousand paths to destruction.'

A new voice piped up. 'Let us try, father!'

'So? My youngest children, the Sprites of the Falls. What will you do, my fickle ones?'

'Welcome them in our garden, father, and make all seem fair. Mortals' senses are easy to cheat. We shall offer them food and wine, and beguile them with laughter. They will drink and forget, fall into a sleep with no waking, and journey no further.'

The voices were growing fainter, and the pillars and balconies began to shimmer as if the whole building were stretching and pulling, drifting off with the current, and longing to be swallowed back up into the water.

'And what if you fail, my daughters?' the cold voice whispered down from above.

'Then the task will be ours . . . ' The voices were swept away as a wind began to blow down the empty corridors that led into the hall. ' . . . wild Sprites of the Streams . . . Hills of Iron and Adamant Cell . . . water all around . . . '

Then the voice of the Worm cut through the whistling of the wind. 'Let it be done. And you, Eldest, and the Sprites of the Springs, return with me to my house, and we shall abide what follows.'

There was a rustle of movement and a sound of scales rasping on stone. The wind blew stronger, and Charlotte looked up to see the walls of the dome swaying and fading. Bubbles streamed past, and a greenish glare swept over the clean, white stonework. She tried to run, but her feet sank into the floor as if it had suddenly turned soft and boggy. She sensed bottomless depths opening up beneath her; in another moment she would be slipping endlessly down into emptiness.

She looked desperately round. By her side was a dim corridor, where the white light still clung. She darted towards it, and slipped down the shadowy passageway just as the domed hall was swept up in a roar of water and whirled away into nothingness.

CHAPTER 11

Death's Head

David and Prince Roland were meanwhile being driven further and further into the Tarn, plunging and slipping down the perilous stair with the storm blowing ever harder behind them. David felt dazed and sick; he kept turning and calling Charlotte's name into the darkness, but the wind took his words and forced him on, down and down, with only the gale to be heard and nothing to see but the gleam of the steps as they rose from the murk in front of him. Down and down he flew, as if in a dream, until at last he heard a shout from up ahead, and stumbled after the Prince on to the bottom of the Tarn.

They gazed around, and then David pointed with a shudder.

'Look! Bones!'

It was true. Ahead, white shapes were flitting through the darkness, ribs and skulls and dead hands, turning and staring and clutching as the gale of mud hurried them unceasingly on.

'Be of good courage,' said the Prince. 'We have naught to fear from the dead.' He led the way forward, and David followed, staggering in the wind. Soon they made out a darkening in the gloom ahead, and found themselves confronted by a dense thicket of dry, crackling thorn bushes, twined together into a solid barrier which stretched high above their heads. There was nothing to do but turn along its edge and look for a way past. They trudged forward, keeping their eyes on the matted wall of thorns at their side. All at once they came to an opening, and then they met a sight which made them blink.

Through the dark tangle of trees they saw a garden. A perfect lawn and brightly coloured flowers shone in a brilliant summer sun, and graceful trees arched overhead, motionless in the warm air. Beyond the lawn there was a white-painted pavilion, and a peacock paced in front of it, piercing the silence with its eerie cry.

The pair of them stood and stared, and then Prince Roland turned to David.

'What think you? Some trick of the Sprites?'

'Maybe . . . but let's take a look anyway. Charlotte might be in there.'

So they advanced into the garden. Now the gale of mud was left behind, and heavy summer scents were all round them. Everywhere David looked the colours glowed almost too bright to be real, as if they belonged to some feverish dream. The peacock's throat shone bluer than the sea, and then it spread its tail, and a hundred flashing eyes shimmered with emerald and purple and gold.

He glanced aside, and caught his breath in horror. In the corner of his eye he saw the peacock transformed into a dingy-coloured crab, scuttling away across grey sand. He looked again, and there was the peacock strutting on the brilliant grass. He darted his eyes from one thing to another, and now he saw that everything in the garden wore two faces. When he glanced away, the white latticed pavilion was a house built of bones; the maples and beeches were brown clumps of swaying seaweed, and bright-eyed eels floated among their fronds where birds had sung a moment before.

He turned to the Prince in panic, and saw his companion gripping his sword and turning this way and that.

''Tis a den of sorcery,' growled the Prince. 'But empty seemings can do us no harm. Come!'

They crossed the lawn. The peacock's call echoed in the drowsy air, and with every step they felt more as if they were walking through a dream. In front of the pavilion there was a sundial, its brass face glinting in the sun. David paused to stare at the inscription which ran round its edge.

'In this shifting land of dreams, nothing's ever what it seems,' he read out. The Prince stopped and looked at him. Both strove to think, but a cloud was settling over their senses. When they glanced once more round the garden, they could see nothing but bright lawn, flowers, and trees, and the words of the sundial seemed without meaning.

Just then, they heard a sound from the pavilion, and looked up. Gone was the house of bones, wrapped round in clinging seaweed: now they saw only white fretwork and painted lattices, with luxuriant creepers growing up the walls and over the roof. The door stood open, and out of it floated the sound of laughter.

'See who is in the garden, sister,' came a voice from inside. A figure appeared at the door, a woman dressed in white, who smiled and held out her hands.

'Come!' she called. 'You have journeyed far, and are weary. Come, eat and drink, and forget your toils.'

David and the Prince hesitated, and the figure in white laughed again.

'Trust to your eyes!' she sang. 'Is not all here pleasant, and all without dark and wild? Come and rest. You can journey no further at present.'

The figure turned, and her feet seemed to glide through the doorway without touching the ground. A great tiredness came over David and Prince Roland, and they followed her dumbly into the pavilion.

Inside, they found themselves in a circular room with windows all round, and a closed door in the wall opposite them. Two more ladies reclined on a couch with their feet tucked under them; their hands were to their faces, as if to check the silvery stream of laughter that rippled through the room. When they saw the newcomers they rose from the couch, and the tallest of the three slid towards them with her hands extended. A smile was on her face, but the hand which David took was as cold as ice. It was pulled away at once, and their hostess beckoned them forward.

'You are welcome,' she said. 'You have braved much. But here are no ghosts or gales, or dangers of any sort. Rest, and refresh yourselves. Eat, drink, and forget.'

She motioned her guests to a pair of richly carved and gilt couches. Lion masks ornamented the couches' sides, and their legs ended in golden clawed feet. The upholstery stretched like the skin of a beast, and David's couch let out a low and distant-sounding growl as he sank into it. The ladies laughed.

'Take no notice!' the tallest cried merrily. 'Sleep, if you will. All is safe.' The forms of the three ladies swam round the room, bright and indistinct, like shapes in a dream. Tables were brought, their marble tops resting on supports like squatting giants, which grunted and shifted their limbs when bowls of fruit were set on top. Then David heard the clink of metal, and looked up to see one of the ladies smiling down on him, and pouring out a goblet of wine.

The fruit-bowl in the corner of his eye had begun to swarm with mice and rats, crawling and squirming over each other, and what had been stems were now tails; but David hardly noticed. He was gazing at the shining face above him, and the purple stream that flowed from a great golden jug in the shape of an eagle. Its beak was the spout, and a faraway cry blended with the chuckle of the wine as it swirled into a silver cup, wreathed with snakes.

'Drink,' came the voice, and the cup was lowered into his hands, the snakes hissing softly and twining round his fingers. 'Drink, and forget.'

The ladies' laughter flowed over his senses. He longed to share in it, and to forget all that was dangerous or troublesome. But still there was something he strove to remember. 'Charlotte . . . ' he began.

At once the laughter ceased. The three ladies were frowning at their guests. Outside the sun had gone in, and a cold wind blew through the pavilion. The words fled from David's mind, and he only yearned for the ladies' laughter to return. The figure before him smiled.

'Drink,' she said. 'Drink and forget.'

The words came floating to David through a great silence and emptiness, as if nothing else was real, not the couches and tables, nor the garden or pavilion, or even the trees and the blue sky overhead. But the words were solid, and up and up they rose through the raging waters and shifting shapes of the Tarn, to where Charlotte was hurrying down a dim, sloping corridor.

The spell of the great domed hall had passed; her wonder and curiosity had gone, and now she only felt alone and afraid, and desperate to find David and the Prince. Then came the words, and they struck a chill through her.

'Drink, and forget!'

She broke into a run. The words of the Sprites of the Falls came back to her, and she muttered over and over as she ran, 'Sleep with no waking . . . journey no further,' until it became a refrain to keep her from slackening her pace.

The ghostly corridor curved down and down. Sometimes it swayed like the deck of a ship, and sometimes it slipped away altogether, and she found herself floating downwards on the current, with a small white house and a brightly lit garden far below, shining through the murk like a rainbow in the midst of a storm. Then she was running again, and the voices and laughter of the Sprites drifted up to her through the floor and walls of the passage.

'It is a cup of sleep,' came the gentle voice. 'A cup of forgetfulness. Come, drink!'

'No!' shouted Charlotte. 'Don't drink!'

Her words echoed down the corridor, and were snatched round and round by the current, until all the empty halls and shadowy rooms of the Tarn were whispering and repeating them.

Down below, David had the cup to his lips. 'Don't drink . . . don't drink . . . ' came the words. All at once he thought of Charlotte and lowered his cup. Prince Roland did the same, and the three Sprites frowned.

'If you do not drink, how can you forget?'

David felt sorrowful and lost. He knew that he had only to drink and the laughter would return; he could forget his sadness and rest. He raised the cup once again.

Charlotte ran with all her might, and now the voices of the Sprites sounded loud and close. Ahead, the passage ended in a door with a bright light shining from under it.

'You do right,' murmured the voice. 'You will find it a soothing draught.'

The walls of the passage flew past her like smoke on

the wind, and then Charlotte had reached the door and wrenched it open.

'Stop!'

David and Prince Roland froze with the cups at their mouths; the snakes darted forward with sparkling eyes and stabbing tongues, and the three Sprites turned to face Charlotte.

'It isn't real!' she shouted. 'They're Sprites, don't you see?'

All at once the golden summer light went out. A biting wind blew through the walls, while tables, floor, and ceiling, fruit and wine and goblet, all were swept aside in a dark surge of mud and bones. The Sprites let out shrieks of rage, and shot away through the water with a flash of silver.

Then Charlotte was shaking David by the arm and slapping the Prince's hand, clenched white over the hilt of his sword.

'Prince Roland! David! Wake up!'

David stared in front without understanding. The laughter and light had gone, and all around him was roaring darkness and cold. His only thought was that something beautiful had passed away forever.

'Was it . . . a dream?' he asked at last.

'Near enough,' said Charlotte. 'It wasn't real, anyway. This is what the bottom of the Tarn is really like: just mud and bones. Come on! Do come on!'

She urged them forward, and David and Prince Roland stumbled after her, their limbs as heavy as lead. On they trudged in single file, with the wind moaning in their ears. Choking swirls of mud eddied past; then a greenish gleam of light would sift down from above, and they could see pale shapes tumbling in the current, the bones of the drowned.

114

'Death's Head,' said David.

'What say you?' demanded the Prince.

'The mud and bones,' David explained. 'It's like Death's Head in alchemy. It's the dregs—what's left when all the rest is boiled away, all the colours and shapes and tastes, all the beauty and life. It's the body of things: what they're made of. Just like everyone's bones are the same once they're dead.'

'I wish you hadn't started talking about death and bones,' said Charlotte. 'Look up ahead.'

Before them through the murk they could see a faint cluster of shapes. They floated motionless in the raging waters, and more were drifting into sight all round. Soon there could be no mistake. Pale hands stretched out to them, and misty bodies began to circle them round. Charlotte turned to her companions with a shiver.

'Ghosts!'

CHAPTER 12

The Adamant Cell

Closer and closer the ghosts pressed round them, stretching their hands out as if begging, while all the time clouds of mud and bones went whirling through their empty forms. Pale fingers stroked the travellers' clothing with a touch too light to feel, while blurred, misty faces gazed into theirs with expressions that could not be read.

'Back! Back!' The Prince slashed around him with his sword, but the ghosts only clung closer, and as fast as a misty shape was swept in two by the Prince's blade it drifted together again, and floated silently up to besiege the party afresh.

Then, suddenly, the ghosts fell back. Their empty bodies writhed aside, cringing before a new arrival. It was a ghost like them, but taller, brighter, and more solid-seeming. Its eyes were wild, and its mouth was drawn back as if in a scream. David and Charlotte knew at once the ghost of the drowned girl that had rushed past them in the tunnel, and Charlotte whispered, 'Jenny!'

The eyes burned into her, and then the ghost turned to its fellows and pointed a pale arm imperiously into the distance. At once, the other ghosts scattered, flitting silently away into the darkness. Then the ghost turned to them with a look full of sadness and pleading, and beckoned them to come on.

Prince Roland hung back. 'Nay, 'tis a trick,' he growled. 'Ghosts and Sprites, all mean our ruin.'

116

But Charlotte was gazing into the ghost's eyes. 'No,' she said. 'She means us no harm: I'm sure she doesn't. Can't you see? She wants rest. If we kill the Worm, the whirlpool is supposed to stop, and then her bones can be in peace.'

They all gazed at the spectre, which stared back with a look of desolate longing. Then it turned, glided ahead, and waited for them once more, shining through the shadows like a beacon.

'Very well,' rasped the Prince. 'I like it ill, but—lead on.' He raised his sword before him, and the three of them advanced towards the wavering form. When the ghost saw that they were following, it turned its sad face aside and once more slid off ahead. So they went on for some time, with billows of mud and bones whirling all round them, and their guide hovering like a pale flame always just in front.

Then suddenly everything changed. A white light pierced through the shadows, and the wind fell. The ghost vanished like a candle in daylight, and all at once they found themselves walking over a bare, rocky hillside, through air that was frosty and still.

Charlotte gasped, and Prince Roland swung his sword; but there was no foe in sight.

'Just another illusion,' said David. He kicked a loose stone over, and they heard it ring like steel on the frozen ground.

'Oh!' Charlotte had stopped. 'I'm trying to remember—it's something I heard the Sprites say, about Hills of Iron. I don't think this is a safe place to be.'

'Yet we are in it,' said Prince Roland, 'and must tread the path before us. Come, the spectre has shown us our course. Whatever false seemings we be shown, we have naught to do but hold firm.' He led the way briskly forward, striking across the hillside in a straight line, and the children hurried after him, blowing on their hands to keep warm.

In a few minutes they came to the brow of the hill. Ahead lay only more hills, rugged and broken, with never a tree or a house in sight. Prince Roland frowned, and then went on, his sword held high. Soon they dropped down into a valley strewn with boulders. They were just beginning to thread between them when they heard a rumbling boom from above, and a torrent of water came shooting down from rock to rock, bounding across their path and swirling away down the hillside.

They jumped back out of the way, and a fountain sprang up from the stream with a taunting face floating in its midst.

'You are fools!' the voice hissed. 'Why did you not choose sleep in the house of my sisters? They were gentle, but we are wild.'

The Prince sprang forward, and swung at the face with his sword. The water flew apart with a peal of laughter, and where there had been one fountain now there were three, bubbling and playing along the length of the stream.

'Let us pass!' commanded the Prince, and three watery faces laughed back in derision.

'The Prince wishes to pass!' mocked one.

'Aye, let the Prince pass!' jeered the second.

'To his death,' finished the third.

Prince Roland faced the Sprites in fury, and would have charged forward in another useless attack, but the streams burst apart into myriad faces and shapes, babbling and rushing all round them. 'Wild!' whistled the voices. 'Wild! Wild! Let them pass! Let them pass!'

They hurried on along the path, and now the Sprites came shooting after them, rolling and snaking over the ground like watery serpents.

'The Prince dislikes our Iron Hills!'

'He will not stop for our Adamant Cell!'

'But little he knows who dwells within!'

''Tis no concern to me,' growled the Prince, striding along faster. The white light was growing faint, and hints of muddy clouds blew across their way.

'Come on!' shouted David. 'The illusion's starting to fade: there's nothing to worry about now!' They broke into a run, while the Sprites streamed past them like arrows of water, leaving hissing swirls of bubbles in their wake.

'Beware!' yelled the first, and the others took up the chorus, whisking round them as they ran, like wasps searching for a place to sting.

'Beware the grove of swords!'

'The maze of curses!'

'The beast with many heads!'

'The thing with mirror eyes!'

'Beware! Beware! Beware!'

'Lies!' shouted the Prince. 'Empty words, that signify nothing!'

Shadows were gathering around them, but up ahead the white light still shone clear, picking out a shallow stream with a great black rock rising up in its middle. There were two openings in it, one at its base and another near its top.

'Beware, beware the Adamant Cell!' shrieked the Sprites, circling round and round, while the Prince lashed at them angrily with his sword, and the children ran hard to keep up. Just as they were about to pass the rock, a shrill voice cut through the air.

'Roland!'

A woman's arm showed at the high opening, and then a face.

'Princess Melisande!' Prince Roland came to a sudden halt, then leapt forward, splashing through the stream at the foot of the rock.

'Wait!' called David. 'Are you sure . . . '

'Beware of visions, seemings, tricks . . . ' sang the Sprites, shooting to and fro round the Prince's head.

'Nay, 'tis you who would trick me,' shouted the Prince, and plunged forward into the darkness of the cave. David was close behind, and Charlotte came after him.

'Wait, wait, do wait!' she cried, trying all the time to remember what she had overheard in the great domed hall. 'The Adamant Cell . . . '

'Empty words!' retorted the Prince. All three were now in the cave, and again the voice echoed down from above, calling on the Prince by name. They looked up. For a moment they saw the pleading face and outstretched arms of Princess Melisande, lit by a brilliant white glare; then the light dimmed, and the vision was swept away in a swirl of mud. Prince Roland stood dumb, while rippling laughter flowed all round the rock.

'Poor fools! Poor fools!' sang the voices of the Sprites.

'Run!' shouted David, but before they could reach the way out a door swung shut with a clang that dinned round and round the cave, and three gleaming shapes swooped down on them from above.

'Now you are lost! Now you are ours!'

'He braved our threats, for a bride of clay!'

'And his journey ends in our Adamant Cell!'

The Sprites circled them three times, laughing and taunting, and then shot up through the high window leaving them in darkness.

CHAPTER 13

The House at the Eye of the Storm

Outside, the gale of mud was howling round the rock, droning like an organ in the narrow window high above. David and Charlotte paced round the walls, seeing their way by the thin ray of greenish light that filtered into their prison. Prince Roland squatted on the floor, eyeing the two children drearily.

'Mine is the blame,' said the Prince. 'Had I but taken time for thought . . . '

'But that was their trick,' said David, 'to fluster us with threats that sounded false but were really true. It was clever.'

'Anyway,' said Charlotte. 'Now what?'

'Now . . . nothing,' said the Prince in a low voice. 'Adamant is the strongest of all material things. My sword of bite would shatter against it. Had this been a prison of stone, or iron, we might yet have won free.'

'What if it's just another illusion?' suggested David.

'What difference?' the Prince replied. 'We are prisoners just the same.' And he tapped his sword lightly against the adamant wall, which gave a sharp, metallic ring.

'And it's not an illusion,' said Charlotte. 'At least, I don't *think* so, because the funny white light's gone, and there's mud and bones again outside. And they're what's real down here, don't forget.'

'I don't know what's real and what isn't any more,' put in David. 'We think the illusions are all made of Death's Head, don't we? And when they fade they turn back into mud and bones again. But according to the alchemy book, everything's made of Death's Head anyway. In fact,' he went on, with a curious glance at the Prince, 'that's how we made this whole world.'

Prince Roland looked up at the dark shape that was David. 'What say you, child?'

'That's true,' said Charlotte, wrapped up in thoughts of alchemy, and ignoring the Prince. 'We made it from Death's Head and Mercury—and the book, of course.'

'Your speech is a riddle,' said the Prince. 'Are you sorcerors? In truth, the storm smelt of witchery. I come nigh to believing that you were the wizards that conjured it.'

'The storm did work pretty well,' admitted Charlotte.

'And it was lucky we remembered who Jove was, or there'd have been no lightning,' added David.

Prince Roland stared, and then he laughed. 'So! But here is a further test for your powers: can you free us from our prison?'

'That might be difficult,' sighed David. 'We left most of our alchemy behind. We've only got three things with us—and no book.' He felt in his rucksack, and pulled out the two sealed glass bottles labelled Shape-Changer and Alkahest. 'And then there's this,' he added, getting out the large, outlandish egg. 'It's got some sort of strange writing on it: "Noli . . . me . . . frangere",' he read.

'That's right,' Charlotte agreed. 'And the book said it was the egg of a cockatrice.'

Prince Roland looked up in dismay. 'Know you not what thing it is you hold?'

'The book didn't say any more than that,' said Charlotte.

'You make me marvel! Nay, I am no scholar of arcane

matters, but I possess at least common learning. Down perilous stairs, through roaring gales you have borne the egg of the most feared of beasts!'

David looked at the egg in his hand. 'And the writing?'

'Naught but plain Latin, and you would do well to heed its meaning. "Do not break me," the egg proclaims. With one slip a thing more deadly than the Worm itself would have been hatched among us. Children, how come you to know so much and yet so little?'

'They don't teach Latin at our school,' said David.

'Or mythological beasts,' Charlotte added. 'Why's a cockatrice so dangerous? It can't be very big.'

'It is the king of serpents, and the fruit of a monstrous birth. 'Tis hatched from a cock's egg, wrapped about in a snake's coils. The very look of the cockatrice oozes with venom strong enough to kill.'

'Well, it might be useful yet,' said David, bedding the egg in his rucksack with extreme care. 'But now we've got to remember all we can about the other two.'

'Alkahest,' Charlotte mused. 'The book called it the Great Dissolvent . . . something like the strongest acid.'

'That's right!' cried David. 'The Alkahest will dissolve anything in the world back into its first matter—into Death's Head. Charlotte, we're saved!'

'And what keeps it in its vessel?' asked the Prince, sounding unconvinced.

'The seal of Hermes,' replied David. 'But we won't go into that. The point is, we can use it to dissolve the adamant.'

'I have told you,' said the Prince wearily. 'Adamant is the strongest of substances. Nothing can break or dissolve it.'

'It's like the immovable obstacle and the irresistible force,' Charlotte reflected. 'Something has to give, but which will it be?'

'Adamant *must* still be made of matter,' insisted David. 'And that means it's got Death's Head in it. If it's made of it, it can be turned back into it. Everything can be dissolved, just the way everything that's alive can be killed. I know I'm right. Watch!'

David raised his arm and threw the bottle at the door of the cell. The glass shattered, and then the dark surface of adamant began to seethe and steam. Its surface crumpled and withered like dying leaves, and in seconds a hole had opened up. Inky strands dripped from its sides like melting tar, to be snatched away by the current and whirled into the roaring storm of mud outside.

'There!' shouted David. 'I told you!'

The Prince jumped to his feet with a cry of delight. 'I shall doubt your powers no longer! Nay, here was a deed to put Mortagon himself, the King's Wizard, to shame! Come, my young sages, let us go on!'

He grasped his sword confidently once more, and bent low to follow the children through the tattered gap in the prison wall. Outside, the river had gone. There was no sign of the Sprites, and the gale once more howled round them fiercely. Then David pointed, and some way off they saw the wavering shape of their ghostly guide. Prince Roland shivered, and hung back.

'Would that we might pursue our way alone!' he murmured. 'But strange companions for a strange road. Spirit, lead on!'

As he spoke, the ghost glided off ahead into the shadows, and the three mortals followed. The ground sloped downwards, and they began to pass through a wood of stark, dead trees. Black branches creaked in the wind, and stiff twigs caught at their clothing like skeletal hands. The gale was blowing stronger with every step they took, and soon the children had to cling to the trees to avoid being blown off their feet. At the crest of the hill the wood came to an end, and the ghost halted.

The pale arm was raised, pointing. Just beyond the foot of the slope there was a ring of trees, and behind it there stood a house. Tier on tier and tower on tower it rose, with all its windows dark. No breath of wind stirred in its eaves, and the trees that encircled it stood without moving.

'The House at the Eye of the Storm,' whispered David.

Prince Roland was gazing at it. 'And there dwells the Worm.' The ghost lowered its arm, and began to pace backwards, staring all the while at the three humans with doleful eyes.

'Are you going?' asked Charlotte, between kindness and fear, and the ghost nodded slowly.

'I thank you,' said the Prince, glancing at the ghostly face and then away again. 'You shall have rest, I promise. Aye, rest and revenge, poor spirit!'

The ghost of Jenny backed slowly into the shadows, fixing them with her eyes until the dark clouds blew between and blotted her from sight.

Then Prince Roland leant into the wind and advanced down the slope. The children took a deep breath and plunged after him. The gale nearly bowled them over, and they broke into a run, feeling as if they were flying on the wind. Ahead, the Prince's cloak was blowing about him, and beyond him loomed the trees, clothed in leaves of shimmering silver that hung motionless from their branches. On David and Charlotte ran through the gale, and then suddenly they saw the Prince stagger, and his cloak slump around his shoulders. The children caught him up, and they too stumbled and reeled. One moment the gale was roaring and tearing at their bodies, threatening to lift them away like flotsam, and the next there was no wind at all. They had come to the eye of the storm.

When David regained his balance he glanced up at the trees and let out a cry. 'Oh! They're not leaves—they're swords!'

As he spoke, there was a clangour of steel like an army going into battle, and all round the house the trees bristled with swords, brandished in the air by arms of wood.

'It was true, what the Sprites said,' whispered Charlotte. 'A grove of swords . . . and what else? A maze of curses, a beast with many heads and mirror eyes . . . and they were right about the Adamant Cell, too . . . '

'Fear not,' said the Prince. 'Here is no sorcery, but only fair fighting. Come, I shall prove to you that my valour is the equal of your spellcraft!'

He sprang forward. A great din of battle arose, as Prince Roland parried a score of blows at a time, slashing and hacking at the trees, lunging and dodging, until arms and swords flew like brushwood, and the ground was littered with limbs, their wooden fingers twisting lifelessly in the air.

'He's doing it! Oh, he's doing it!' cried Charlotte, clapping her hands. But now they heard a new sound over the ring of steel against steel. There was a slow, heavy tread, and a whistling hiss; the swords parted to make way, and a monstrous shape slid out from among the trees. A sinuous neck writhed up from the shadows, and then another and another. Soon a tangle of heads was swaying over the Prince, their jaws yawning and snapping, showing flickering black tongues and teeth of iron.

The Prince took a step back, but still faced the monster dauntlessly. He poised his sword, glancing from one head to another, and scanning for some opening. Then one of the heads leant forward, hissing and staring, and the Prince's eyes were caught. He stared back, fixed by his own reflection, wavering and helpless. His sword slowly fell, while the beast crept forward, and its other heads began to snake round, ready to take him from behind.

'The thing with mirror eyes!' cried David. 'Prince Roland! Don't look into its eyes!'

The Prince shook himself, and darted back just in time as a pair of heads snapped at him, one from each side. Now his anger was roused, and he sprang to the attack. The heads writhed aside, arching high and slithering along low, and Prince Roland lashed at first one then another; but whenever his sword was about to strike home, the heads before him melted away into the air, and others sprang from the creature's body like fresh flames leaping from a fire.

'It's *not* a fair fight!' insisted Charlotte. 'David, what can we do?'

'It's all right,' said David slowly. 'It's an illusion. You'll see: if he can't hurt it, it can't hurt him.'

But he was wrong. The Prince flailed ever more desperately at the vanishing heads; they faded away before his eyes with mocking smiles, while others crept round behind. Now one bit into his mail shirt and dragged him to his knees, and another fixed its jaws into his arm. Prince Roland let out a cry, and lashed out; but the head turned to smoke before he could hit it, and another pinioned his sword arm.

128

'David! David!' cried Charlotte. 'What are we going to do?'

They had retreated step by step as the beast crept on, and now David felt himself snatched backwards off his feet: without knowing it, he had stepped back into the gale. Over and over he tumbled through choking clouds of mud, until at last he found his feet and crawled back into the area of calm, battered and dizzy. Charlotte ran up to him.

'Oh, come! Quick! Do something!'

'My rucksack: where is it?'

It had fallen from his shoulder close by where the Prince was struggling in the coils of the monster. David ran back for it, his mind desperately working through recipes for alchemy. He reached out his hand, then snatched it back. Something in his rucksack was moving, wriggling and squirming to be free. There was a raucous squawk, and a head like a rooster's appeared, followed by a snake-like body.

'Run!' shouted David, and dragged Charlotte after him into the gale of mud.

'But—' Charlotte glanced back at the Prince, and caught the barest glimpse of the red, burning eyes of the cockatrice. She fell panting beside David, shaking and flushing hot and cold.

Mud whirled between them and the Prince, still fighting in a tangle of snaking necks and heads. One of them had him round the waist, and others were winding behind him, when the cockatrice slithered out and sat up on its coils. A snake's tongue hissed from its cockerel beak, and again its squawk rang out. Its gaze swept over the Beast, and where its burning eyes passed, heads withered and sickened like dying plants. The Prince let out a cry as the deadly stare touched him, and sank among the ruin of shrivelling, steaming heads. Then the cockatrice looked beyond, taking in its new world; its eyes rested on the grove of swords, and wooden fingers curled in agony with a clatter of steel as the swords fell from their grip.

The Beast meanwhile roared from every throat and turned in rage on the cockatrice. Heads ebbed and flowed, shooting out and vanishing like flames; but the cockatrice stood its ground, and turned the full scorching glare of its eyes on the Beast. Heads screamed and sickened, blackening and swelling with poison; but all around came more, and now the cockatrice was caught in their mesmerizing stare. Eyes of burning red gazed into eyes of glaring silver and, reflected deep in the Beast's mirror eyes, the cockatrice met its own deadly stare. Just as the poison flowed round the jaws and nostrils of the Beast, and its eyes grew dim and lifeless, the cockatrice opened its beak and let out a terrible, dying shriek. The fire went from its eyes, its beak clacked shut and open in a silent gasp, and its snake-like body fell dead and shrivelled beside its foe, wasted by its own poison.

Only three heads were left to wave triumphant over the body of the cockatrice. The curling jaws smiled in victory; but the venom was in its veins. The Beast's body lay smouldering in decay. As David and Charlotte watched, blackness travelled slowly up the last three necks, which swayed and fell hissing and steaming to the ground.

The children lay shivering with horror, and then they heard a groan from beyond the remains of the Beast. They got up and ran from their hiding place.

'Prince Roland!' called David. 'Are you hurt?'

'Nay,' grunted the Prince, 'I have but a gash in my

arm. But the look of that thing—the eyes of the cockatrice—they burnt into me like coals. Nay, come,' he said, crawling slowly to his feet, 'I shall do well enough. Let us go on.'

He still held his sword, which he had not sheathed since the night of the storm, and led them falteringly towards the trees. On either side the swords waved menacingly, but directly ahead the cockatrice's look had scorched a safe passage through the grove. They picked their way past the bare, blackened branches, while underfoot they tramped over rusty blades which flaked away at a touch, still hissing and steaming as if they had been worked on by some powerful acid.

'That egg did us proud after all,' remarked David, and the Prince turned a haggard face in his direction, and smiled faintly.

Beyond the trees they came to a halt. Behind them they heard the clashing of swords as the trees strove to reach them, and from further off still came the raging of the storm; but ahead all was silent. The great, dark mass of the House at the Eye of the Storm rose over them, gaunt and brooding. Windows stared down like the empty eyes of a skull, blacker even than the black rock of which the House was built. In silence, they paced round the outside of the walls, gazing up at the towering roofs that were never shaken by any wind.

At last they halted beside a great doorway, standing open like the mouth of a beast gaping for its prey. The three exchanged looks, then gathered their courage and advanced into the darkness. They could hear nothing but their own footsteps and the sound of their breathing, and at first their eyes were blind. Soon, however, they found that there was a faint glimmer of light, no more than a greying of the darkness, but just enough to see by.

They were in a great hall of pillars, which clustered all round them like forest trees, and offered them murky vistas off into the shadows. Soon they came to a place like the crossing of several paths through a maze, and they stopped and listened. In the deep quiet, there was a faint swish, and then again. They craned around in all directions, and then David pointed silently down one of the avenues between the pillars.

'What was it?' whispered Charlotte.

'I don't know—something glittered. Like a great fish.'

'See!' cried the Prince.

Far off in the gloom, something was moving, like a train of sparks, or a stream of water caught by the sun. Left to right it passed, then right to left, closer each time. Next they saw the great head of the Worm flitting across the avenue and passing quickly out of sight, with its glistening coils pouring after it. The yellow eyes reappeared, and the Thing swam straight towards them.

The sight seemed to put fresh strength into Prince Roland, who drew himself up ready to face it. But the Thing veered aside at the last moment, and they heard its voice echoing through the hall.

'Prince Roland!' it hissed. 'You come unasked. Why do you disturb my peace?'

'You know my errand,' shouted the Prince back. 'I have come for Princess Melisande, whom you stole.'

'I?' murmured the voice, and again they saw the flash of its scales as the Worm circled and circled, threading through the maze of columns. 'But she is mine, Prince. Your father sold her to me for his life. Perhaps he is the thief, and not me?'

The scaly body whisked past close by, and the Prince whirled round, slashing at the water with his sword.

'You lie!' he cried.

'Perhaps I do,' whispered the Thing. 'Why should I not?' The voice came to them fainter now, resounding from far off through the hall. 'Your father was lost; the price was set, and he paid. Now you are lost too, Prince. And what will *you* pay me that you may live? Nay, you do not have the price. You are lost, and you must die.'

The dragon's words echoed down the pathways of the maze, and silence fell once more. Prince Roland still peered into the darkness, wheeling all round, his sword at the ready.

'No!' he shouted. 'It is you who will die, Foul Thing! Fight me! Come and fight!' But his words died away in the silence unanswered.

'It's not quite time yet,' said Charlotte, tugging at his sleeve. 'Don't worry: it'll have to fight soon. In the meantime we've got to find our way through this maze.'

'You speak well,' admitted the Prince at last, lowering his sword arm. 'We shall go on. Keep by my side, and no harm will befall you when we come to battle. Come!'

He strode off into the shadows, and the children followed close behind, peering from side to side down the ever-changing views that opened up between misty ranks of pillars. After a while, Charlotte let out a gasp, and the others turned.

'Look! Don't you see? Some of the pillars have walls built in between!'

It was true. As thin as silk and as dark as the shadows themselves, a web of solid partitions was woven from one pillar to the next, turning the hall into a labyrinth of different ways and turnings.

'So it *is* a maze,' said David, following his sister's eyes round the dusky passageways that branched off on every side.

'Then we must hurry through it and come to our goal,' said the Prince. He turned and strode on, and when the children looked round he had gone.

'Oh!' gasped Charlotte. 'Prince Roland! Prince Roland!'

'Here am I . . . ' His voice floated eerily down the corridors, and the children turned this way and that straining to hear where the voice had come from.

'Over here!' cried David.

'No, here!' Charlotte contradicted.

'Follow!' echoed the Prince's voice, and now it sounded as if it came from all around them, and was welling out from the shadows that stretched away in every direction.

'It's no use!' Charlotte cried. 'We've lost him!'

CHAPTER 14

Shape-Changer

'Come on,' urged David. 'He can't be far away. Hurry!' He set off quickly down one of the passages, following the direction he thought Prince Roland's voice had last come from.

'But I was sure it came from back there,' protested Charlotte, and at that moment they heard the Prince again, from off to one side, and, as it seemed, higher up.

'Fight me!' echoed the voice. 'Come, Thing, and fight!'

The words drifted and rebounded, sounding from this side and then that. Just then, they came to the foot of a staircase, wedged in between two pillars.

'Up,' said Charlotte. 'His voice came from somewhere up above.'

They set off at once to climb the stair, which wound and wound around one of the pillars. They were in total darkness. It was cold; their breaths hissed, and their feet slapped on the stone steps. Then they heard another sound, a kind of mournful music that came throbbing through the walls and welling up from the stone all around them. Soon they could hear it more clearly. It was the sound of a sad woman's voice singing, accompanied on a harp. The voice hung in the air like perfume, and still they climbed in the darkness.

'Light!' gasped David, and they came out on a landing, where once more they could see their way by a dim, greyish light. The singing was louder now, and seemed to be coming from a narrow window up ahead. Charlotte led the way across to it, and together they peered out. They were looking down on a high, dome-shaped room, and Charlotte thought at once of the great house of illusions that had formed in the waters of the Tarn.

Far below, a woman was sitting alone among brightly coloured cushions and tapestries, singing and playing on a harp. A brilliant white light was dancing over her, and glinted off her golden harp, which was surmounted by a gilded figure of a bird on the wing.

'Is it a Sprite?' whispered David.

'I'm not sure . . . do you think it's Princess Melisande?'

David grunted uncertainly, and they continued to stare below them. As they did, they heard the sound of steps, and Prince Roland entered the room, still with his sword drawn. When he saw the seated figure, he ran forward a few paces.

'Princess Melisande!'

The figure stopped playing, and looked up at him with a smile. 'No, it is I: Eldest.'

'Eldest!'

'Yes, my Prince. You see, there is no deception.'

'No, I warrant there is none,' growled the Prince. 'You would have slain me!'

'I! Slay my Prince? Not so, I swear to you.' And she gazed unblinkingly into his eyes until the Prince turned away in confusion.

'You see I bear you no grudge,' the Sprite went on tenderly. 'But why did you stay to watch us dance in the storm, when I bade you go? Nay, it was not well done, my Prince. Water is wild, and you saw what you should not have seen. When the wind blows, we must follow:

136

we have not the power of you cold mortals to curb our natures.'

'But—you would have drowned me!' gasped the Prince, and indignation wrestled with the evidence of his eyes as the Sprite smiled unfalteringly up at him. High above, the children were clutching each other in impatience.

'He's going to believe her!' whispered Charlotte desperately.

'No he's not. Let's listen.'

'Drowned you!' echoed Eldest lightly. 'Yes, I would have drowned you. My poor fool! If you had kissed me, you would have been one of us, and danced with us in the wild wind, to the storm's singing. In truth, I would have drowned you. Do you not see that your old life must die before the new can be born?'

'But the ghosts,' objected the Prince, and now he looked as if he was drowning indeed, in a sea of words and arguments that flooded his mouth and lungs, choking the life out of him. 'The ghosts, and the bones at the bottom of the Tarn! Come,' he said, regaining some of his confidence, 'what say you to that?'

Eldest threw back her head and laughed. 'Country clowns! Fools who slipped on the rocks, oafs in love with their own faces in the water, silly maids who drowned themselves for a cowherd's love. Would you have gone the way of such as they? And did I promise any of them my favour, and ask them to join the dance on the waters? Nay, my Prince, I think not.'

The Prince said nothing, but lowered his sword to the ground and looked down.

The children in their vantage point groaned, and both at once began to scream and call the Prince's name. But the sound of their voices echoed thinly round the hall, dwindling as it fell, as if they were in a dream, straining to shout their loudest, and no sound would come. The Prince did not look up.

'To dance in the wind,' murmured the Sprite, 'to be water dancing on water, cold in the coldness, darkness in the dark of the night . . . Things are seldom what they seem: what appears fickle may be constant. But mankind never trusts more than its eyes can see and its fingers feel.'

She turned away with a toss of disdain, and the Prince raised his head and looked at her in silence. She caught his glance in the corner of her eye, and then she smiled.

'Nay, come,' she said. 'If you will not join our dance, you shall even so have my help.' She sprang to her feet, and flicked aside the corner of a rug which was covering a grille in the floor. The white light flooded down into a cell below, and Prince Roland sank to his knees with a cry. 'Melisande!'

The prisoner stretched her hand up to the bars with a cry, and for a moment their fingers met. Then the light faded, and their hands slipped apart.

'Take this,' said Eldest, and tossed an iron key into the Prince's hand. 'You have the key, and you have seen her prison, though neither will avail you until my father is dead.'

'Your father?' gasped the Prince.

'The "Foul Thing",' replied Eldest. 'I am a traitor to him. And will you not grant me your trust in return? I have offered you all I have to give.'

The Prince was turning the key over and over in his hand, and then he looked up again into the face of Eldest.

'Come, my Prince, we must hurry if we are to take him unawares. He cannot be killed by steel: I must take you to the place and show you how to do it. Come: will you trust me or will you not?'

Prince Roland stared at her for a long moment, and then he said, 'Yes, I will trust you.'

High above, the children groaned in agony, and screamed and shouted until they were hoarse. But their voices were lost in the emptiness of the hall. In a moment, they fell silent, and watched with horror as Eldest glided up to the Prince.

'Give me your sword,' they heard her murmur. 'It will be of no use to you now. For do you not know that my father can only be slain by a charmed blade? Take this, and leave your sword behind.'

As if bewitched, the Prince let the sword be taken from his grasp. It dropped on the floor with a clang. Then his fingers closed around the hilt of a curving dagger, and he followed Eldest dumbly from the room.

'Hurry!' shouted David, and made for the stairs.

'Wait,' said Charlotte. 'It's like the dome in the illusion . . . Let's try over here.' She led the way to an opening closer to the wall of the dome, and soon they were tripping down flight after flight of stairs, along parapets and balconies and landings and then down once more, until at last they tumbled the last few steps on to the floor of the cavernous room.

They glanced around in bafflement. Where there had been embroidered cushions and draperies, now there were only dirty billows of mud, and in place of the harp there stood a cage of bones, with a skull set where the bird had been.

'Can this be the same place?' wondered David.

'Yes, it is!' shouted Charlotte. 'Oh, look! Look!'

There on the ground lay Prince Roland's sword, partly hidden under a great stain of mud.

'Lies!' burst out David, and kicked the bones over into the murk. 'Now what are we to do?'

'We don't know which way they've gone,' said Charlotte, glancing around at the six doors which opened off the room. 'And even if we did, we'd never find them in the maze.'

'If only we had the alchemy set!'

'Oh, David, there's one piece of alchemy left! Have you got it? Is it broken?'

David fished about in his rucksack and drew out the bottle. The thick old glass was still sound, and vague forms churned and swam inside.

'Come on,' said Charlotte. 'We've got to think! Shape-Changer. What can we do with it?'

'The book called it a spirit. Like the Mercury we made that brought the world to life.'

'Yes . . . and, oh, David! A spirit, and Death's Head—they're body and soul—if you put them together, you get something real!'

'Well?'

'Look!' She pointed to the wafting cloud of mud that hovered around the heap of bones. 'There you are: Death's Head!'

'So if we add this to the mud,' said David slowly, 'we'll get something real . . . something living?'

'Yes,' insisted Charlotte. 'The Shape-Changer.'

'And that is . . . ?'

'Do it, and we'll see! It's our only chance!'

Without saying another word, David lifted the bottle and flung it to the ground in the middle of the cloud of muddy water. There was a whoosh and a boom, and the children staggered back, dazzled by light. Then they crept forward again, gazing in fascination on the shifting mass of shapes and colours that writhed and twisted before their eyes. Sounds and voices of every kind screamed and whistled and hummed round the room, as the Shape-Changer formed mouths and muzzles and maws, grinning, yelling, trumpet-shaped. Hands and feet, hoofs and paws shot out from it, only to be swallowed back into a churning mass of shapelessness.

'What now?' demanded David. 'How do we control it?'

'I don't know,' said Charlotte, and as she spoke the squirming heap of shapes began to stretch and grow, and take on a definite form. Four paws sprang from a tan body, followed by a head and a whisking tail. The shape bulged and swayed; a last human hand sprouted from its side and was swallowed up, and then a dog shuffled up to them, panting and snuffling at their hands.

'David! I thought of a dog! That's how you control it!'

'Quick, then!' David reached for the Prince's sword and held it out by the blade. 'Here, boy! Sniff! Seek!'

The dog fell to sniffing at the hilt of the sword, and then it sprang off into the darkness down one of the passageways that led from the room.

'Come on!' shouted David. 'And keep thinking of dogs!'

So they ran, and they each thought about dogs as hard as they could. They thought of shaggy dogs and bald dogs, brown dogs and black dogs, and their guide went through some very strange changes as they ran; but he never lost the scent, and in a few minutes they came out into a long, vaulted hall. Quick footsteps echoed through the stillness, and far in the distance they could see two figures almost disappearing into the darkness, and behind them a pair of dark shapes gliding stealthily after them through the water.

'The other two Sprites,' groaned David. 'What are we going to do? All he's got is a dagger, and it's bound to be a fraud. We'll never catch up, and the dragon might appear at any moment!'

'Then it had better be now. David, think of the dragon!'

So they both concentrated on the Worm, and the panting dog was swallowed up in a whirl of changing shapes. Then, with a chilling hiss, a wrinkled, scaly head rose up from the blurred mass. Its sly, yellow eyes stared right through them, and its tongue flickered round its iron teeth. The whole length of its glittering body poured out of the shifting heap of colours as if from the door to another world, and shot forward along the murky corridor. The tip of its tail took the last of the Shape-Changer with it, and then there was only the Worm, the Thing that dwells below, snaking over the stone floor and hurtling down on the Prince and the Sprite.

David and Charlotte ran their fastest, while the Prince wheeled round to face his foe, clutching the dagger which Eldest had given him. The two Sprites of the Springs cowered out of the way, and Eldest turned to the phantom Worm with a look of surprise.

The mighty jaws gaped, and Prince Roland sprang forward to the attack. He raised his dagger and lunged at the side of the Worm's head. But before the blow struck home the glittering blade dimmed, and the charmed writing that ran along the dagger's length faded. Then blade and hilt dissolved into mud, and oozed out between the Prince's fingers to fall in gobbets to the floor. The Sprite behind him let out a low sigh of pleasure.

The Prince stepped back in bewilderment; he cast a brief, questioning look at Eldest, then reached for his sword; but his scabbard was empty. The Worm rested its eyes on him. A smile danced around its jaws, which opened to receive their prey.

The children were meanwhile running up behind at full pelt.

'Think of . . . a sword!' panted David, and all at once a blob of colour shot out from the side of the Worm and landed in Prince Roland's hand. He took no time for thought. His sword was in his hand, and his enemy was before him. He raised his arm and struck.

'My father!'

Eldest flew forward with a scream, as black blood boiled from a ragged wound on the side of the Worm's head. Its yellow eyes rolled, and its snake-like tongue lapped out around the great teeth. Its claws scratched along the ground, and the Prince struck again and again, until the blood welled out like a fountain. Now the other two Sprites rushed forward and joined their screams to those of Eldest.

'You promised no harm would come!' wept Eldest. 'You promised! I gave him the dagger as you bade me!'

'And what of your promises to me?' roared the Prince, turning on Eldest.

Eldest faced him with a look of fury, and at that moment the children ran up.

'Don't worry,' panted David. 'Your father's not dead—yet. Look!'

The twisting body of the Worm, writhing in its death-throes, began to blur and change. Its eyes faded, its coils withered and shrank, and its scales lost their gleam. In a few seconds there was nothing left but mud.

'What—' gasped Eldest. 'What is this?'

'It's a trick,' stated Charlotte. 'You know all about them. We've beaten you at your own game, that's what.'

'Here's your sword,' said David to the Prince. 'Your real sword.' He handed it hilt-first to the Prince, who was gazing in astonishment at his hand, left for the second time clutching a ball of mud.

'You'd better be going,' Charlotte told the Sprite. 'I don't think you're wanted here any more.'

Eldest turned in rage from one hostile face to another; then she swept herself up in a whirling tornado of bubbles and foam, and shot screaming up through the water with her two sisters following after.

CHAPTER 15

A Fight in the Ruins

Prince Roland was balancing his sword in his hand, and looked in wonder from the children to the muddy mass that had been the phantom dragon.

'Once again you have saved me,' he said. 'I begin to see of how little use a sword can be.'

'That's what we told you at the start,' said David. 'But just keep hold of it: it's going to be lots of use soon. Come on, let's find the Princess!'

They made their way back along the dusky corridor, and soon came to the great domed room, with its litter of mud and bones marking the spot where the Sprite had deceived the Prince.

'And is her prison here, below our feet, or was that too an illusion?' Prince Roland asked. They searched over the whole chamber, and then the Prince let out a cry. The children ran to his side, and there was the iron grille, buried under a caked mass of mud.

'Prince Roland!' came the cry from underground, and the Prince tremblingly searched for the lock, the key in his hand.

'We're coming!' Charlotte called back, and then the key turned, and Prince Roland heaved up the iron door with all his might. Still without speaking, he reached down, and pulled Princess Melisande out by both arms. A slender figure stood before them, dressed in a soiled white gown, her fair hair matted around her face with the dirt of her prison. She smiled into the Prince's face as he kissed her hand, and then she noticed the children.

'I had no doubt you would come,' she said to Prince Roland. 'But who are these, your companions? Were they too prisoners of the Worm?'

Prince Roland laughed. 'Nay, no prison would hold them! These are my wizards, who have saved me many a time by their spells, and can judge the true from the false without fail. Is it not so, my young sages?'

'Well, *mostly*,' admitted Charlotte. 'But then, you see, we'd read the book, so we knew what was going to happen. It's a long story.'

David coughed, and addressed the Princess. 'You don't, perhaps, know the way out, do you?'

'Yes,' agreed Charlotte, 'because the dog we made came to rather a sticky end, and we've no more magic left, you see.'

Princess Melisande gazed at them with wide eyes, and then she smiled. 'Indeed, dear sages, I know something, though not enough. I have heard the coming and going of the Sprites through the maze, and they have a rhyme by which they guide themselves right.'

'Can you remember it?' asked Charlotte breathlessly.

'I can. When they would leave the House, they repeat as they set off:

'Thrice to the left and twice to the right;
thus may you pass from darkness to light.

'But through which of these six openings they then depart, I know not.'

They gazed around the dome-shaped room, and prowled along the walls searching for some way of telling the doors apart. Part way round, the Prince gave a cry, and stooped to the floor.

''Tis the mark of my sword, where I let it fall!'

The others crowded round. 'Then this is the way you came in by,' said David. 'Well? Shall we try it?'

Prince Roland gave a nod, and they set off into the maze. At the first turning they went left, and then twice more. The pillars rose all round them, and seemed to whirl and dance as they threaded their way rapidly through the winding passages.

'Now right,' said the Prince as they reached the next turning, and Charlotte noticed a mark like a curled snake on the pillar by their side. Right, thrice left, twice right, and left again once more; on and on they wandered in the dim silence, and still there was no sign of a Sprite, or the Worm, or the door of the House. After some time they began to be worried.

'We've gone wrong,' said David. 'We must have done.'

'It is most probable,' replied the Prince. 'The shadows lie thick: how may we count the turnings without error? But we can only go on.'

They came to a turning, and by their reckoning it was time to take their third turn to the left. Suddenly Charlotte stopped.

'Wait! It's that funny mark again!'

'What's that?' David demanded, coming back.

'The mark like a snake,' she said, pointing. 'When we passed it before it was on the first turning to the right. It could mean that again!'

'Well, we're lost,' said David. 'We might as well try.' He looked around at the others for agreement.

'You are lost,' murmured the Prince, remembering the words that the Worm had spoken, first to his father the King and then to himself. 'Nay, young sages,' he added aloud, 'I shall trust to you: guide us!'

So Charlotte led them down the right hand passage,

and then right again, three times left and then right, and at the last turning they passed another of the coiled snake marks.

'There!' she cried in triumph, and now they went on with new confidence, peering carefully around them so as not to miss a turning. Soon they could feel no walls between the pillars, and knew that they had come out into the echoing hall where they had first met the dragon. The way led clear through the forest of columns, and they broke into a run.

'We're out!' shouted Charlotte, as they left the gaping doorway behind them, and emerged into the green, flickering light of the bottom of the Tarn. They skirted round the House to the gap in the Grove of Swords, and passed between the menacing arms back into the raging of the gale. They ran on, huddling their heads against the storms of mud that boiled around them, and soon were struggling up through the barren wood and into the Hills of Iron.

'There are no Sprites,' David marvelled. 'No illusions, no Worm. It's letting us go without a fight!'

'Not so,' replied Prince Roland. 'It will choose its time. When we are on the stair, then will our defence be weakest. But let it come: I shall welcome it!'

They pressed on, and still there was no sign of anything at all but swirling mud and rattling bones, and sometimes a ghost that flitted aside before them into the shadows. Before long they could see the rock wall of the Tarn looming ahead, with the Winding Stair slanting up its side, level upon level. At the foot of the stair David turned to look back, and drew in his breath sharply. Far away through the water he could see a shape snaking rapidly towards them. The others halted, and followed his gaze.

'Go on!' commanded the Prince. 'I shall come after, and make ready to meet our foe.'

The children set off up the stair, pressing themselves close to the wall and forcing their way against the gale. Then came Princess Melisande, and lastly Prince Roland, looking out all the time at the sinuous shape that came whirling towards them through the storm.

Suddenly it was upon them. The yellow eyes swept by in a blur, the jaws gaped, and the head darted and snapped. A clawed foot swung past their faces and rasped over the rock. The children heard the clang of the Prince's sword. He parried and slashed, but always the Worm slipped back in time, and the rocky overhang prevented it from coming at him from above or behind. Then with a snarl of rage it lashed its tail and was gone. The water seethed and churned after it, sending skulls and ribs rolling and spinning in the eddies, and they saw the whole train of its coiling body whisking after it, with pair after pair of gnarled legs trailing underneath.

'Now what?' breathed David.

'It will come again,' replied the Prince. 'Its wrath is roused, and it will not be thwarted by aught save death.'

But it did not come. Far off in the murk the beast was circling, while the four humans crept slowly along the rock wall, with their faces into the wind that was always pressing and urging them back the way they had come.

For a long time they climbed, and then in an instant the scene changed. They were plodding up a steep path in single file, winding their way up a grassy hillside under a leaden, overcast sky. Princess Melisande caught her breath in alarm.

'It's just an illusion,' Charlotte reassured her. 'We're still on the Winding Stair, really. Just keep going.'

So they kept on. From off to one side they heard the sighing of the sea, and soon they came out on an open hilltop. The path had disappeared.

'Now where are we?' demanded David. On three sides stretched the sea, lifeless and grey, while bare hillsides rose inland, fold on fold. Ahead, on a crag overlooking the sea, stood the shattered ruins of a castle.

'Beltenebros,' murmured the Prince.

'But it's not,' said Charlotte. 'Look!' She pointed into the distance, where through the sea-haze they could just make out row upon row of winding stairs, slanting up the side of the Tarn.

'It's all the way round us,' Charlotte went on. 'We're not on the stair at all: the Thing's tricked us!'

'Come then,' growled the Prince. 'If the Worm dares to fight, let it fight.'

He led the way forward to the ruins, his sword held high. Ahead stood King Stephen's castle, gutted and abandoned, its halls empty, its towers crumbling. They advanced slowly towards the barbican. Its mighty walls had been thrown down, and only the arched gateway remained, with tottering stacks of masonry standing forlorn around it. Prince Roland shuddered, and paused before entering.

Suddenly the Worm was on him, snaking out from the broken archway like some thing of the deep from the wreck of a galleon. The Prince's sword whirled and struck, shielding him from teeth and talons and the coiling, crushing body that came writhing and pouring round and round him, flashing like a cataract of water.

Then the glittering stream of scales uncoiled and flowed off into the shadows. The Prince reeled, and leaned against the arch, panting for breath. In a moment he staggered to his feet, and led the way into the castle.

The drawbridge was gone, but they crossed the moat on a bed of fallen masonry. The courtyard was desolate and overgrown, with broken walls rising around it. Halfway across, the Thing came on them again. Princess and children scattered, and once more the glittering body flowed round the Prince and the great head yawned and snapped over him. Then it slithered away again, and vanished through an archway. This time the Prince's mail was torn and his helmet gone, while his sword was still unbloodied.

'The cowardly thing!' cried Charlotte. 'Why won't it stay and fight?'

'If only it wasn't so quick,' said David bitterly. 'It's playing with him. Wearing him out.'

The Prince was swaying as he walked, but still he followed after the Worm, through the archway into a roofless space that had once been the great hall. Ferns grew from the crumbling walls, and the broken pavement was covered in moss. Prince Roland stared around in sadness, and then passed through into the kitchens.

'Here we played as children,' he murmured. 'Do you remember it, Melisande? See how 'tis gone to ruin.'

But the Princess had begun to weep, and the children looked with alarm at the tired form of the Prince. Then from the door that led to the tower the Thing was on him again. Round and round it flashed, while the children cowered in one of the great hearths. It writhed aside, and now the Prince tottered on his feet, a wound showing through the torn mail on his arm. The Thing was crouching before him like a cat waiting to spring, and the children saw the look in its eye, almost human, which had stayed King Stephen from striking at it in the forest. The Worm slid slowly forward for the kill, a smile spreading round its jaws.

For a moment the Prince stood still. Then he tore his eyes away from the Thing's hypnotic gaze, and lunged at it with the last of his strength. His sword flashed forward. Rage and amazement showed briefly in the Worm's yellow eyes, and then it let out a hissing roar of pain and whirled into the sky, trailing a dark streak of bloody water from its throat.

Prince Roland sank to his knees, and the illusion began to dissolve. The greyness of the sky faded, and a greenish light played over the ruined walls, making them look like some sunken city swallowed beneath the sea. Above, they saw the Worm doing a dance of death, twisting and snapping its body in agony like a whip.

The children and Princess Melisande ran forward to the Prince, who was heaving deep breaths, still kneeling where he had struck the Worm.

'You killed it,' David could only say. 'You killed it.'

Princess Melisande pulled him tearfully to his feet. He looked around and managed to smile, then he wiped his sword, and slowly slid it into its scabbard.

' 'Tis done,' he breathed.

'But we're not safe yet,' said Charlotte. 'Look.'

The ruined walls were growing dark, blurring and losing their shape. A gust of wind blew past, and the towering masonry began to break into drifts of mud that swirled away in the current.

'Quickly,' said David. 'We've got to get back to the stair!'

They struggled out into the courtyard, but their feet were dragging in the ground, now black and soft like peaty quicksand. Beyond the barbican they could go no further. Their legs were held by the wallowing blackness,

152

while the ruined town stood out white and bleak below, a gathering of skulls on a hill of mud.

Above them, the dragon's dance was almost done. It twisted and flailed, and then it came plummeting down on them, its blood pouring after it, stirred into a spiral by the current. The curling shadow covered them, and the dying eyes fixed on them as it came; then, just as they would have been swept down into the depths of the Tarn along with the writhing body of the Worm, the last of the grey light faded, and a swirl of water swept them and the whole murky hillside out from the dragon's path.

Down and down the Thing sank, its body turning slowly in the current, and its blood poured after it into the darkness. A dappled, shifting light began to fall from above, dancing over the wall of the Tarn in a pattern of colours. The whirlpool slowed and then stopped, and they all four swam towards the stair through water that was clear and still.

CHAPTER 16

A New Ending

Wearily they climbed the last part of the Winding Stair, while the flickering shapes of sun and clouds called to them from above. David was the first to burst from the water out into the air, and he stood on the ledge blinking and drawing in breath after breath as the others came up behind.

'I'd almost forgotten it,' Charlotte panted, gazing round at the brilliant yellow of birch leaves mirrored in the Tarn, the sharp line of the trolls' crag, and the cold blue of the evening sky. The air felt as pure and sharp as springwater.

Then David suddenly remembered something. He reached into his rucksack for the great mother-of-pearl cup with the dolphins and mermen gambolling round its sides, and laid it carefully on the rocky ledge above the steps.

'There,' he said. 'Helga ought to find it there. I expect she'd like to have it back. I wonder if she'll ever manage to make herself beautiful?'

'Maybe one day,' said Charlotte with a frown, 'but I still think she's got a long way to go.'

Prince Roland cast rather a puzzled look at the children and the cup, and then he smiled and took Princess Melisande's arm. 'Come,' he said. 'There is the cave of the ghosts yet to pass.'

He led the way into the tunnel, and the Princess shivered and closed her eyes. They hurried past the glowing finger-marks of the ghosts, and soon were out once more in the cold evening air. Princess Melisande heaved a long sigh, and hung on Prince Roland's arm, and the children too let out deep breaths of satisfaction.

'That's that, then!' commented David, as they began to make their way round the Tarn and back towards the village.

At this, the Prince turned to them with a curious look. 'Children,' he said, 'I have followed wherever you led and done whatever you bade me—I, a prince. Now, children, tell me truly. Who are you? Whence do you come? And what knowledge have you of things hidden from the eyes of others?'

'Well,' Charlotte began, 'your wizard Mortagon said we were spirits from a purer realm, and that's sort of true.'

'We call it the real world,' put in David, while Prince Roland and Princess Melisande exchanged baffled looks.

'We couldn't bear for you to be killed,' Charlotte went on. 'We just couldn't. But the book said you would be. It was a made-up book, and the only way of stopping it was to make it real—make it true. No one in your world knew: and no one else in ours could get into yours.'

'Look, these are the pages,' said David, holding out the tattered pieces of paper that had started their quest.

'Nay, I shall not read them,' said the Prince, drawing back. 'If they be true, I would not be told what Fate had willed for me. Do with them as you will.'

'Well, they're not true any more,' said David. He ripped the paper into shreds and threw the pieces behind him.

'We made all this,' explained Charlotte, gesturing at the rocks and trees around them, 'using an alchemy set. We made it from Death's Head—from mud and earth—just like the illusions in the Tarn.'

'Nay, that passes belief,' the Prince objected. 'Below the Tarn were lies, feigned shapes and airy phantoms, given body by sorcery and conjuring. But this ground on which we tread, this air, this sun, our flesh itself, all are real and solid things, if aught is.'

'How do you ever really know what's real and what isn't?' queried Charlotte darkly.

'You too may hail from a world of dreams and phantoms,' put in Princess Melisande, giving the children a sly smile. 'How might you say it was not so? You are no more real than we to look at.'

'Oh, of course you're real *now*,' David assured her.

'Only now?' queried the Princess, the twinkle in her eye growing brighter. 'Nay, not even in earliest childhood do I ever remember being otherwise.'

'But it was still us that made you that way,' retorted David, growing confused himself.

At this Princess Melisande clapped her hands and laughed. 'A rare pair of elves! I believe they are spirits in truth—tricksy and subtle, and delighting in riddles!'

They were coming through the hollies at the foot of the wood, and had been so wrapped up in their talking that they had not heard the confusion of sounds from up ahead. Then the trees parted. They stopped at the stile, and stared in wonder. The fields before them swarmed with activity. The ground as far as the stream was dotted with brightly striped tents. Pickets and sentries, cooks and horsemen came and went between them, to the sound of clashing armour, tramping feet, and bellowed commands.

They advanced down the path, and soon were met by a challenge.

'Halt—who goes? By the King's beard, 'tis the Prince!' The man-at-arms turned back to the camp, shouting the news as he went. Prince Roland smiled at his companions, and led them on into the camp. From all around the soldiers flocked. Face after face, haggard and worn from hard marching and worry for their prince, broke into smiles and cheers and shouts, until the children thought the din would deafen them. On they went, to a great tent in the centre of the camp, with purple draperies hanging round its mouth. As they approached, a white-haired figure emerged from inside, blinking in the light, and staring about to find the cause of the commotion. It was King Stephen.

Then he saw the smiling faces of his son and his ward coming on through the crowd. The old King's face froze in amazement, and then it broke slowly into the closest it could come to a smile, and tears came into his eyes. His hands reached forward from the thick fur cape he wore against the cold, and then he clasped the Prince and Princess in his embrace.

David and Charlotte stood and watched, while the men in armour roared out their cheers all round, and hammered their sword hilts on their shields. From out of the King's tent rushed the pages, Peregrine and Guy and Walter and Oliver, waving their arms and cheering louder than anyone. They clung to the children's arms and danced round them, and then David and Charlotte felt a level gaze fixed on them. Beyond the King stood the tall figure of the wizard Mortagon, hovering in the shadow of the tent like a dark flame. Suddenly the wizard, too, smiled, and then nodded his approval.

'Aye, my children. Whether you be spirits or no, my art fails me to determine; but your warning was heeded.'

'What! Mortagon! The children, aye, the children's warning,' the King broke out, catching sight of David and Charlotte past the Prince and Princess. 'Aye, for a day we brooded and did naught. But Mortagon judged you to be messengers of truth and not falsehood, and, as I think, he judged you right. But what has passed? What of the Worm?'

'Dead,' said the Prince. 'But indeed it would have been I that perished, but for these children. Nay, 'tis beyond my fathoming how they came by their knowledge.'

'Did I not say so?' burst out the King. 'Ha! Did I not, Mortagon? They are wise prophets, our children. But why came you to a king for aid? You needed it not!' And King Stephen's smile cracked a fraction wider even than before. 'Come now, come,' he went on, bustling forward from the tent. 'Let the scouts be called back, and word be spread that all is safe. Evening is drawing in: we shall feast and be merry, and hear of your spellcraft, children, hey? And Mortagon shall be your apprentice!'

The soldiers cheered, and David and Charlotte followed the Prince and Princess into the royal tent. Trumpets blared, summoning all the villagers and men of the camp for the feast. The children sat beside the King, and they could hardly eat for all the toasts in their honour, and the many questions they were asked about their home and their adventures.

At last the fires burned low, the stars twinkled and flashed in the frosty air, and the minstrels fell silent. The children slept warm and safe in a tent close to the King's, and when the yellow morning light woke them they could not at first remember where they were. Their adventures came back to them bit by bit, and then they thought of home.

'It's time to go back,' said Charlotte, and David nodded.

'Mum'll be worried sick.'

'Well, there's no need,' said Charlotte indignantly. 'We can look after ourselves perfectly well.'

They got to their feet and stepped out of their tent, where they met Prince Roland. All around was the bustle of tents being taken down and men-at-arms preparing for departure.

'We strike camp,' said the Prince. 'Whither would you go now?'

'To a hill south of Beltenebros,' answered David, 'where there's a rope hanging from a hole in the sky. That's how we get home.'

'But first we have to go back to the holly thicket for something,' added Charlotte. She led her brother off from the camp, while Prince Roland stared after them.

'The alchemy set, you mean?' queried David.

'Of course. It's got plenty more in store for us yet.'

They soon found the hollow under the holly trees where they had camped, and dug about in the leaf litter until they unearthed Charlotte's rucksack with the alchemy set beside it. By the time they got back, the army was almost ready to leave. They breakfasted with the King, and then they were mounted on ponies, and set off down the Wandering Valley at the head of the army.

The villagers cheered them off. All that day they rode, joking with the pages as they went, or discussing alchemy with Mortagon; but mainly they kept close to Prince Roland and Princess Melisande, and listened to them talking of their past and their plans for the future.

The Giant Rodomont cowered in his castle as the army passed joyfully by, and in the evening when they camped there was more merry-making and story-telling. The next day they rode on. In the early afternoon they came within sight of the sea, and the gleaming turrets of Beltenebros.

'Not a ruin, after all!' sighed Charlotte, remembering the vision in the Tarn with a shudder.

At the edge of the town the children hung back, and cast longing looks up at the hills.

'And may you not tarry?' urged the King. 'Nay, return with me to my court, and be my wizards. I shall not lose you; nay, I shall not.'

'But we have to go home,' insisted Charlotte, and Prince Roland spoke from the other side.

'Let me guide them, father. It is right they should have their wills.'

'Well, so be it, so be it,' grumbled the King, turning his horse aside with a frown. His place was taken by the wizard Mortagon, who spoke to them swiftly and softly.

'You promise well in magic; but you are young, and the road to mastery is long. I beg you to accept a gift of me, and may you prosper in your art.' He reached into his saddle bag and handed them a book bound in leather, with a tangle of symbols engraved over its surface in gold. The children thanked him in surprise, and with a last secret smile the wizard turned away.

Now the army was passing on into the town. Princess Melisande embraced them, and Charlotte tugged at her sleeve.

'You will look after Prince Roland, won't you?' she begged. 'Sometimes he needs a bit of help.'

'You may trust me for that!' laughed the Princess. 'Now fare you well in your strange land above the sky!'

She turned and was gone. Then Prince Roland led them up the path into the hills. The sea sparkled in the afternoon sun, and the children gazed all round as they went, taking in every detail of the world they were about to leave. The Prince kept them company in silence until they came to the track where they had met the old woman gathering sticks. They roamed for some time among the mossy rocks and twisting oak trees, before seeing what they were looking for.

There ahead was the rope, hanging down as far as the forest floor and reaching up above the tops of the trees. Overhead it vanished into a dark opening, which hovered in the brilliant blue of the sky like a stain on silk. The children turned to the Prince, with no words for their goodbyes.

Prince Roland smiled at them, and held out his hands. 'Farewell, my young elves. My thanks go with you, whoever you be, and whithersoever it is that you go.' Then he glanced up at the opening in the sky, and turned away again with a shiver. 'But mean you in truth to ascend through yon gloomy portal? Attempt it not, I beg you.'

'We really have to get back home,' insisted David.

'To that real world of which you spoke? Nay, children, you are flesh and blood, just as I. Remain with me: journey not to that dark place of spirits hanging in the sky.'

'We've got to go,' said Charlotte. 'But first promise us that you'll live happily ever after. Otherwise what's the point of changing the story?'

The Prince smiled again. 'I promise you I shall. What should hinder me, now that I have my bride?'

The children looked into Prince Roland's face one last time, and then they stepped up to the foot of the rope. David went first, and then Charlotte, gripping the knots with their feet. Up they crept past the treetops. Below, the rope swayed, and the Prince stood underneath, gazing up at the dark passage out of his world.

Soon David came to the opening, and the metal of

the cauldron rang hollowly as he grasped the rim and pulled himself up. He jumped out on to solid ground, with Charlotte following close behind. It was dusk. Sunset still glowed in the sky, and the first stars were just coming out. Beyond the canal, traffic was roaring on the ring road. Charlotte glanced down again into the cauldron, where the autumn afternoon still shone, chilly and bright, and then turned to her brother with a worried look.

'How long have we been away, David? I mean, we spent a good few days inside the book. Have we been gone that long, or no time at all?'

David was frowning at the charred sticks round the base of the cauldron. 'I don't know. The fire's gone out. That's a bad sign.'

Charlotte said nothing. She coiled the rope and tucked it under her arm, and then they threaded their way through the weeds to the path and set off home across the park. There were not many people about.

'There ought to be signs up to tell people what day it is,' said Charlotte. 'What does your watch say?'

'It stopped, when we went down the Tarn.'

'Mine did too.'

At last they came in sight of home. There was a light on in the sitting room, and another in the hall. David pushed the door open, and Mum and Dad appeared at once.

'Where have you been?' Mum burst out, staring at their walking boots and rucksacks. 'Why are you dressed like that?'

David and Charlotte shifted uncomfortably. 'We haven't been gone . . . long, have we?' said David.

'Long!' Mum repeated. 'Almost two hours! Your tea's stone cold!'

162

David let out his breath. 'That's a relief,' he muttered.

'That's *what*?'

'I mean,' David floundered, 'it might have taken us a lot longer.'

' "It"?' repeated Mum. 'What?'

'What you told us,' put in Charlotte, coming to her brother's rescue.

'What *I* told you?'

'You said we should give that book a better ending. So we did.'

David was pinching Charlotte's arm to make her be quiet, and at that moment Dad noticed the coil of rope she was carrying.

'With my tow rope?' asked Dad.

'With lots more than that,' Charlotte assured him.

'And I see you had to put knots in it.'

'It was the only way,' Charlotte confirmed.

David tugged at her sleeve. 'Maybe we'd better go up and get changed.'

The children edged round their parents and escaped upstairs. A few minutes later they met again in David's room. Charlotte sat down on the bed with a frown. 'Don't they fuss? And that's without knowing where we've been!'

'Don't even think of telling them.'

Charlotte was silent a moment. 'What happened, anyway? It didn't take no time at all, but it wasn't real time either.'

'I've been thinking about it,' said David. 'It's like we said: things in books take time to read, but not as long as they take to live through. *We* spent several days there, but if you wrote it down you could read it all in a couple of hours.'

'But . . . does that mean it was still just a book? We did make it real, didn't we?'

'Of course we did. We couldn't have gone there else.'

Charlotte was still frowning. 'Then there's another thing. You say we *made* it real. But the Prince and Princess can remember things from years and years ago. *They* think they've been there always.'

'Well, we gave the world a past as well as a present. That makes sense, sort of.'

Charlotte drew in her breath. 'And a future, too?'

'How do you mean?'

'I mean, are they really going to live happily ever after?'

David thought a moment. 'We'll read the book! Then we'll know.'

Charlotte smiled, and just then they heard their mother's tread on the stairs. That evening and all next day their parents kept a close eye on them, and David and Charlotte spent a good deal of time dodging awkward questions about where they had been and what they had done.

The day after that was Monday, and after school the children at last made it to the library and searched out a copy of *The Nine Sprites of the Tarn*.

'The picture's the same,' complained Charlotte, as David handed it over to be stamped. The librarian raised her eyebrows.

'Never mind, it'll be different inside,' said David. 'It must be.'

When they were back home and settled in Charlotte's bedroom, together they opened it and read.

'The first bit's the same too,' said Charlotte.

'Of course it is: that's not the bit we changed.'

'David! Haven't you noticed? It's fatter than it was!'

'Not surprising: I expect we added a good few chapters.'

'Look—here's the storm, and here's us!'

'And here's where we went down into the Tarn, and the King's march. It says he was warned by portents.'

'Read out the ending,' urged Charlotte.

David flipped through to the last pages of the book, and began to read.

'"Then the Prince and Princess were married. The King's melancholy departed, and peace and prosperity came to Beltenebros. Now rain falls on the Tarn; its waters are stirred by the wind and flecked in autumn with falling leaves. The ghosts are at rest, and the Worm has passed away into memory and legend. But on a winter's night, when the water mirrors the stars, you may still see the Nine Sprites, wheeling about the image of the moon, water dancing on water, dark in the darkness of the night, and cold in its coldness."'

There was silence. Charlotte let out a great sigh and put *The Nine Sprites of the Tarn* on her desk next to Mortagon's book of magic.

'So we really did it,' she said, and David nodded. 'Well then,' Charlotte went on, 'how about turning some lead into gold?'